JANE ANN KE

Linda-
Thanks so much for buying my book! This is my own "labor of love" and how lucky for me to be living the writer's dream! Always pursue your dreams!

Jane Ann Keil-Stevens

LIES
OF THE
FATHER

Outskirts Press, Inc.
Denver, Colorado

Lies Of The Father
All Rights Reserved.
Copyright © 2011 Jane Ann Keil-Stevens
v2.0

Cover Photo © 2011 JupiterImages Corporation. All rights reserved - used with permission.

Outskirts Press, Inc.
http://www.outskirtspress.com

ISBN: 978-1-4327-6888-1

Outskirts Press and the "OP" logo are trademarks belonging to Outskirts Press, Inc.

PRINTED IN THE UNITED STATES OF AMERICA

DEDICATION

*This book is dedicated to all women who have faced incredible hardship
in their lives and who have shown the world that they can
persevere and survive whatever life throws at them.
Calling them "the weaker sex" is a true injustice.*

ACKNOWLEDGEMENTS

Bill - you urged me to finish the book, when at times, I didn't think I could.

Todd – your praise during the process kept me going.

Toby - you wished me success, and the success was in writing it.

Taryn - you advised me through the business side of the writing.

Barbara - you were my first and best critic.

Bob - you were with me "in spirit" through every step of the journey and I will continue to take you with me on the next one, as well.

Mom - you always wondered if all the hours I spent writing would ever lead to anything – it did.

CHAPTER ONE

She remembered how it started, the day her life changed forever. It was the day that a mother never forgets because of what happened to her child. It was also the day that a wife never forgets because of what happened to her marriage. That very day, it was harder than ever to be Kate Nelson.

Kate could still recite verbatim not only what she said, but what everyone else said, too. They were the words that would be etched in her memory forever. She had always been a very gentle, loving wife and mother, but now even more so in light of recent events. All of a sudden, the loving mother part was taking on a life of its own. She was totally consumed with the trauma it had caused her twelve year old daughter and Kate was bound and determined to protect her at all costs. The loving wife part was more complicated.

In the beginning, it was all hearsay, confusion and speculation as to what had happened and the details were sketchy at best. Everyone was pointing fingers and guessing what went on, but nobody knew for sure. People like to stick their noses where they don't belong, spout off what they think they know, when in reality, they know nothing.

She wasn't able to think rationally because she felt as if the whole situation was an oxymoron. On one hand, here was her daughter Kara saying that her dad was responsible for what happened and her husband swearing it wasn't true. It was the classic rendition of the "he said-she said" thing but this time, she was siding with "Team She-Said" because she believed her daughter. Kara would have no reason to lie, but Don would, if he was guilty.

Kate was going to protect her daughter, period. She believed the words that Kara spoke and at this point, there was no reason to doubt her. Then the police informed her that there was sufficient evidence to arrest Don, which was good enough for Kate. It just wasn't good enough to cement her support of Don through this.

So here she was listening to a daughter tell her what a mother never wants to hear and a husband who had been arrested because of it.

She took Kara in her arms and held her close. They clung to each other for comfort and strength. Neither one of them spoke a single word, but they understood the pain they were feeling and that their world had just been shattered.

CHAPTER TWO

Don Nelson was a devoted husband, father, good provider and an avid sports fan. Now he could add something else to the list: Inmate.

All he knew is that he didn't belong in jail. Why was he brought here anyway? Was it because he gave in to some little misstep in judgment? Possibly, but he didn't commit a murder or anything! They were treating him like the worst of the hardened criminals and he was far from it. The reason he was here didn't matter as much to him as the need to get out. He didn't care who he had to pay or who he had to talk to; he was going to do whatever was necessary. The problem was that the jail officials threw him in the cell, like an animal, and probably assumed he was just another thug who committed a crime and was there to serve his time and wait it out. He wasn't one of "them", why couldn't they see that? Did he act like them? Did he talk like them? Did he have an attitude like them? The answer was no on all counts, and yet here he was among them. He didn't belong there and it was getting increasingly more difficult to try and convince someone of it. All he needed was someone to listen to him, hear what he had to say. It would only take a minute, but even trying to do that much while in jail was next to impossible.

Did they intend to leave him there for hours on end without telling him what was going to happen next, so he'd be prepared? He didn't want to venture a guess; he already knew the answer. His frustration was growing as each minute went by and he started to pace the cell, like in one of those 1950's black and white jail movies. His eyes were rolling back and forth as his stomach turned sporadically and it was making him dizzy looking at the dirty, cracked floor. As he walked that same pattern, the feeling that he was going to vomit grew. Don lifted his fingers and started to massage his head, moving them slowly so as to not miss a spot. The regular throbbing beat was both annoying and painful at the same time. He knew he was in some real trouble. Don thought it best to just lie low for the moment. He didn't want Kate to start putting the pieces together, and knowing exactly what did happen and when. It was in his best interest not to rock the boat, but he wanted to. Kate was so mad at him right now that she wanted nothing to do with him. He really couldn't blame her, if he was in her shoes. One day they were living their happy little life, and in a matter of 24 hours, everything had changed. It had all happened so fast, that he really hadn't had the time to take it all in. It was as if it was a nightmare, instead of reality. The only thing he knew for sure is that it was real, and that's what worried him.

He had only been at the jail a few hours and already his palms were wet with sweat, his clothes were starting to reek of body odor from letting his nerves get the best of him and his mind was playing tricks on him.

Maybe it wasn't just being in jail that was getting to him; maybe it was the fact that the whole thing had been blown out of proportion. He was the only one who could set the record straight, the only one who had the information that everyone wanted to know. He was the only adult who knew the exact details of the night in question and who were they going to believe ---- him or a child?

What he really wanted was a shower.

"Guard, guard?" Don asked, in hopes of alerting one of them to his cell. Finally, he heard footsteps and he was glad he got their attention.

"Do you think I could take a shower?"

"Do I think you could? No!"

"Why not?"

"Because it ain't shower time right now, that's why."

"But I am not asking for all that much, just a shower, a measly shower."

"Look, I don't know what your problem is but you need to learn to keep quiet. We'll tell you when it's time for a shower, and it ain't now. Got it buddy?"

"Yeah, but..........."

"What do you think this place is? A four star hotel? Yeah, you wait here while I go get you the monogrammed towels, too."

OK, so the guard was a real smartass, but even so, Don couldn't afford to get on the wrong side of him, so he figured the best thing to do was just to leave everything as it was. He felt like he was five years old, asking for a cookie.

For the moment, he didn't have a cellmate. He didn't need anyone else around him now, trying to make small talk with someone he didn't care about. Already he felt uneasy and having to tiptoe around someone is just what he didn't need right now. All he wanted was out and it was the only thing he could think about. He kept trying to convince himself that once he had a lawyer, he'd be able to get out of there. Telling himself that was the only way he kept his sanity. He needed something to look forward to, something to keep his spirits up. For now, it served the purpose of keeping his mind occupied with something to wonder about.

He sat on the too thin mattress in his cell, alone with only his thoughts, but he preferred it that way. It gave him time to think about what had already happened and how he was going to deal with what was to come. He was limited as to what he could do from the inside. He sat on his cot and took the mattress in his hands and squeezed it as hard as he could, releasing it and watching it unfold by itself. It was like his life, things were crumbling right before his eyes and there was nothing he could do to stop it.

What he needed was an attorney, and with Kate being unwilling to help him, there wasn't much he could do. Don knew that Kate was already taking Kara's side in this and that meant she wasn't about to do anything to help him. She'd already read him the riot act. If it was proven that he actually had tried to abuse their daughter, their relationship was over, just like his entire life. For as nice as Kate could be, she also had a rough side to her. When that side of her took over, she meant business. He was on a downward spiral, he could feel it, but he wasn't ready to admit it to himself. He kept thinking there was a miracle waiting for him around the corner. That kind of thinking only muddied the waters and clouded his vision of how things really were.

SEXUAL ABUSE ON A CHILD. The charge was as ugly as it sounded. The cops had to be crazy if they thought he could follow through on something like that! He got angry at the thought of someone believing he could actually do that! Who would believe it? Not his friends, who would easily describe him as the "All-American" dad. He was the one who drove the kids to soccer practice and treated the entire team to ice cream after a win. Not his business associates, who had the ultimate respect for him. Not his neighbors, who knew him to be the nicest guy you'd ever want to meet. Could his arrest change their thinking? Could it serve to prove his innocence because the charge was so ridiculous for a guy like him, who was liked by almost everyone? He understood that he deserved to be humiliated and punished for trying to follow through on his disgusting plan. But did he deserve a jail sentence along with the loss of everything good in his life? It seemed harsh, and everyone who had heard about his arrest just assumed he was guilty. There was no opportunity for him to explain his side of what happened. The worst of it was that there was actually no one who wanted to listen to him.

His whole life flashed before him; the life where he was Don Nelson, upstanding member of the community: The life where he was the husband of Kate and the father of twin teenage sons, Tommy and Timmy, and a daughter, Kara. The life where he had a successful career in the financial business, and although he did have to travel quite a bit with his job, he always hated leaving his family. The life where he was satisfied that he was doing his best to be a part of the All-American Dream, which included owning a home in the suburbs and having two cars in the garage. No one would have called the Nelsons rich, but they were comfortable. Giving their kids piano lessons, attendance at camp and the like was not a hardship for them.

Don was starting to feel like a caged animal, one that constantly hits its' head against the side of the glass, trying to get out. Having him locked up here was a mistake. Don would be the first one to admit that he needed a warning after what he had tried to do, but did he deserve all this? He heard rough footsteps approaching the cell. Startled, he jumped off the mattress and stood up to see who was coming down the hall. It was the guard, making his rounds. Don wasn't sure how to approach him, but knew this might be his last chance to talk to anyone for hours.

"Hello?"

"You talkin' to me, buddy?"

"Ahhhh........look, I shouldn't be here. Is there anything you can do to help me? I have to find a way out of here. "

"Well, look around. Everyone thinks they shouldn't be here and they all say it's a mistake. Take it from me, you'll do a lot better when you just relax and take it easy. Ain't no use fighin' it."

"But you don't understand. I am innocent, really. I didn't do what they said I did. It's not fair that I am in here."

"All I can tell ya is to take it up with the judge. I can't do anything for ya, except to try and keep the troublemakers outta here. Now sit down and keep quiet. I've already spent too much time talking to ya."

"But wait!"

"Hey buddy, you got a hearing problem or something? I said sit down and shut up! That's my advice and I suggest you take it. You are starting to get on my nerves, and ask these other guys, I don't like when that happens." Right about then, Don was starting to feel like he would be pressing his luck if he did keep talking. This guy had a short fuse, it wouldn't take much more to set him off and he didn't need that. Any type of blowup in here might look bad for him when, and if, he ever did get out. It seemed as if this was the type of place where you were better off keeping your thoughts to yourself; less chance of being blamed for anything.

Don told himself he would never forget the looks on those around him as the police cuffed him and dragged him through the crowd to the waiting squad car. It was all so humiliating! The people at his office were shocked and just stood and stared at him in disbelief. As the barrage of officers paraded by his co-workers, with him in tow, he felt totally alone and ashamed. The scene was always in his mind and he could never fully get rid of it, but for only fragments at a time.

Don sat on the edge of the mattress staring straight ahead, not concentrating on any one particular thing, his mind adrift. The jail atmosphere was good for that, so far it had lent itself to preventing concentration on anything. In this case, maybe that was good. There was the sound of the constant footsteps of those on guard and the noise level was worse than he ever heard. How would he be able to devote some time to sort all this out when he couldn't even hear himself think?

He was at a loss of what to do next. Every idea that seemed good at first came to a dead end. He thought it was ridiculous that a man with his standing in the community should have to endure this humiliation. So here he was, without a lawyer, without a thought of his own on how he was going to get out of here, and without a clue of how the upcoming arraignment would go if he didn't have a lawyer in time. All he did know is that Kate had refused to help him out by hiring a lawyer for him. Kate told him to get a court appointed attorney, but he wanted a private attorney. She made it very clear to him that she was on "Team Kara" and that he was on his own with his problems and how to fix them. How could she turn on him like that? It was never like this before. Who said they had to be on different sides? Hadn't they been on "the same side" for the past eighteen years? He didn't want a public defender because they were for guys who couldn't afford a lawyer. Everyone has heard the horror stories of those attorneys being overworked and underpaid. What kind of representation could he get from one of them under those circumstances? Those guys were either trying to start off their career that way or trying to prove they were some social work do-gooder. No thanks, he wanted no part of that. He had the money for a private attorney, just not the ability to get one! He didn't want anyone to think he was destitute. Then he realized that in the scheme of things, was that really his worst problem? No, his worst problem was the fact that he couldn't rely on Kate to help him when he really needed it. In fact, there was no one he could rely on. He was totally alone and that fact, if he wasn't careful, was the one that could send him over the edge.

Everything and everyone around him seemed strange and they had a bad "me first" attitude. After spending only a little time there, he could now separate the inmates into two types: those who kept to themselves just waiting out the time they had left and those who were the loudmouth troublemakers and thrived on making the place worse than it already was. They were all so desperate.

Don sat down on the mattress and mulled over the prospect of the upcoming arraignment. He had no idea what was going to happen there and was worried about it. If he didn't have a lawyer soon, he was afraid he might say or do the wrong thing and the thought of his having to stay in jail just made him sick.

What he really needed was a pad and pencil and he had neither. All of his personal belongings were taken from him when he arrived at the jail. He figured asking a guard to get him those was probably use-less and quickly learned that the only person you could depend on in jail was yourself. Your thoughts were the only thing they couldn't take away, they took everything else, including your dignity. The environment made it hard to concentrate, hard to think and the noise level at times seemed intolerable and made his head hurt. Nothing inside this place was easy. His first thought was once placed in a cell, he would have time to read, write, plan his strategy, etc., but that turned out to be wishful thinking. He hoped he'd be out before there was even time to get used to it. That was probably just wishful thinking, and he didn't even want to admit that to himself.

There was iciness about the institution, a feeling that even as summer's sweltering heat was baking the sidewalk outside, this place would never be warm, either in temperature or demeanor. It was almost as if the bright sunny streaks of light were barred from this place; a place which had long ago surrendered to despair. The older men who had been here for any length of time had lost most of their youthful manner and they all had their turn at slowly becoming desperate, unshaven, unwashed and for the most part, all suffered from the "I was framed" sentiment. They felt that they had somehow been wronged by being put in there, even though Don knew that a large percentage of them must have been guilty. They were mostly unkempt men who screamed and pounded the wall with anything they could find just to vent their anger and frustration of being locked up for so long. The younger men were extremely volatile and sometimes just a look from someone could set them off. They were dangerous and Don got that message loud and clear. These were not the guys you wanted mad at you, so he thought it best to ignore them, hoping the guards would keep them in line.

As the day stretched into the evening, Don realized he had done nothing to think of any possibility, no matter how remote, to help himself. How could he? He wasn't allowed to use the phone and he had originally depended on Kate to take care of hiring the lawyer, but now that she told him she wasn't going to help him, he was on his own and left to fend for himself. He could overhear some of the other inmates scheming for the one idea that would set them free of this hellhole. Desperation could make even those with limited ideas think they were on the verge on a brainstorm.

Don was fatigued from the day's ordeal, which had run the gamut of being scared to being ready to break out of here himself. He might have seriously considered it if he could have thought of how to do it and get away with it. All he wanted right now was to get out of here, go home to a nice cozy house surrounded by his family enjoying a hot meal. That's the way it used to be, and the way it still should be. So he made an error in judgment; a huge one. Was that reason enough to treat him as if he had murdered someone? Did anyone get hurt? Physically, no. Mentally, he wasn't so sure. But still, because of that error, did he deserve what he was getting?

There was the constant noise, the intermittent yelling of the guards and the fact that he was tense because he didn't know what was going to happen next. He was worried about who would try to defend him and if a public defender would really be all that interested in his case. That was an awful lot of trust to put in someone he didn't even know. He'd heard some of those horror stories, and now he had his own.

Don was able to doze off for just a few minutes when once again, he heard footsteps. He assumed it was one of the guards making his rounds, but discovered it was someone to see him. Kate? No, not Kate, the steps were too loud and fast to belong to her.

All of a sudden, he was face to face with a guy in a suit and tie, an oddity for this place. The guy extended his hand to Don and introduced himself with, "Mr. Nelson? I'm Ken Higgins. I was notified by the court that you needed me to defend you and I wanted to come down here to meet you personally. Usually, an attorney is assigned to you at the arraignment, but I wanted to meet you before that. Of course, you do understand that you are being charged with trying to sexually abuse your daughter. Is that correct?"

Don replied with, "Well, they are saying that I tried to sexually abuse my daughter, but it's not true! I would never do something like that! I was returning home from a business trip and the next thing I knew, I was arrested at my office and in total shock. When they told me the charge, I was sure they had me mixed up with someone else and all they said was "don't worry about it pal, we got the right guy." It seemed the more I tried to tell them I was innocent, the more forceful they became. I was nervous about continuing on with trying to explain my innocence because they weren't listening to me anyway and then the only thing they said was "tell it to the judge". I asked my wife, who is not my biggest fan right now, to hire a lawyer because it was obvious I was getting nowhere talking to them and didn't want to push my luck and make the situation any worse than it already was. When I talked to her, she said the only one she had decided to help in this was our daughter and that I was on my own. So yeah, I'm in a mess right now and don't know what to do."

"Mr. Nelson, I have been in the legal field for awhile and none of my clients has ever walked up to me and admitted to doing the crime they were charged with. However, a lot of them were proved wrong in court and they ended up going to jail. All I am saying is that I can only defend you on what you tell me and how honest you are with me."

Don answered with a weak, "OK. It's embarrassing that anyone in this world would think I was capable of doing something like this – and with my own daughter!"

"It's just the nature of the charge. Anything along those lines is so troubling for most people and that fact alone will make it difficult. I can't make any promises. I'll only say that I'll do my best. Any lawyer worth his salt would never guarantee the outcome of a case to a potential client, especially before having the chance to review all the details of the case, although that's usually the only thing they want to know. All I will promise is to do the best job I can for you based on the facts of the case. Good enough?"

Don replied with the same, "Good enough". What else could he say? He didn't know this guy from Adam and now he had to put all his hope and faith in him to try and get him released? Don was a little confused and wondered why it would be so difficult to get him out of there if he was innocent, and why everything was happening so slowly. It was as if once you were inside these walls, time stopped. The only thing you knew is what went on in there and that's all you were allowed to know. If you were one of the inmates, you were at the bottom of the totem pole and no one saw a reason to change it or was brave enough to voice it. It wouldn't matter, nobody cared.

"All I ask is that you tell me the truth when I ask you something. If you do, things will go a lot smoother. I can only defend you against what you tell me and if you don't tell me the entire story, I can't help you. Do you understand?"

"Yes, I know."

"You're being charged with some pretty serious stuff, you do realize that, right?"

"I sure do, that's why it must be so hard for anyone to get me out of here and I'm getting really impatient."

"You're aware that you are going to be arraigned in the morning, right?"

"Yes, but can you explain what will happen?"

"Well, it means that you'll be brought before a judge and at that time, you will plead guilty or not guilty. Then, I'm hoping I can bond you out. In other words, we hope the judge will set bail, and usually he will with a first offense. You have never been in trouble before, so I am counting on that fact to help us out, too. If the judge sets bail, you will have to pay 10% of it and then you will be free to go."

"Really? That's great."

"You can never read the mind of a judge. I've had cases where I was sure what he would decide and then he did the exact opposite."

"I understand. Will Kate be there tomorrow?"

"I really don't know. It's really not necessary because the entire time we are before the judge will only be a matter of minutes. The sole purpose of the arraignment is to plead guilty or not guilty. Do you understand?"

"Yes, but that's all I get to say?"

"That's it for now."

"Alright, when do you think I can get out of here?"

"That's something we won't know until I formally ask the judge to set bail."

"OK. I am trying to be hopeful about this, but am worried about it."

"Don't be. Just be truthful and you will have nothing to worry about."

"I will." Don extended his hand in friendship to the attorney and he responded in kind by grabbing Don's hand with a strong grip.

"The jail personnel will escort you to the courthouse in the morning, along with the other inmates, just so you know what to expect."

"OK, thanks."

With that, Ken Higgins left the jail for an evening to be with his own family. On the drive home, he was thinking that this may be a hard case to defend. Once people hear the charge, they cringe over its' disgusting nature. But he'd defend Don as he did any other client, with his very best effort. A client deserved that much, no matter what the charge. The person accused had a right to legal representation, whether he had a strong opinion on the charge or not.

Don was grateful to know that at least he had an attorney, but he was surprised to learn that Ken had never defended anyone on this kind of charge before. With the problems Don had at the moment, he wasn't in a position to argue about who he wanted to defend him. He hoped Ken Higgins could give him the outcome he wanted, but there was no guarantee of anything and that's what made him worry.

So here he was taking a chance with an attorney he knew nothing about. To add to the misery, this attorney had never defended anyone on this charge.

Don wasn't stupid, but no matter how he looked at it, he hated his odds.

CHAPTER THREE

Kate woke up early and realized she was in bed alone. Her usual routine when waking was to open her eyes and see her husband next to her, tousled hair and all. This morning the routine was different. There was no Don lying next to her — only open space between her pillow and his as she faced the prospect of having him remain in jail. Right now, Kate didn't care if he ever came back to the house or to her bed. She was incredibly hurt over what he had tried to do to their daughter and he'd have to be totally crazy if he thought she would welcome him back to the house with open arms, as if nothing happened.

Something did happen and that something was what was keeping her and the kids away from him. She also knew that today was the day she planned to sit down with all three of the kids and let them know how they would deal with all that was going on. They had a right to know. It would be impossible to hide it much longer, and she didn't want them to find out from anyone else. Although Kara knew some of it, her twin sons, Tommy and Timmy, were expected home today from a school field trip and they had to be told. They weren't babies; it was so hard to believe that they were seniors in high school. She hated the fact that they had suddenly been thrown into the world of having a dad who was in jail. That's not the life she wanted for them. In the last few days, everything had changed. This wasn't the conversation you ever wanted to have with your kids. She couldn't imagine how it would be facing them, looking into their cute faces, and telling them that their father was in jail and that the life they had before was all but gone. She had to reassure them that everything was going to be fine. That's what you do for your kids; it's how you protect them, it's how you comfort them. The trouble was, she didn't know if what she planned on telling them would end up being true or not. Who knew if everything would turn out fine? Who knew what would happen when people started to find out that Don was in jail? All she knew to do right now was tell them the truth about their dad and that somehow they would make it all work. Kate wondered if that was true, but she had no other choice in what to tell the kids, she didn't want to scare them by saying otherwise. She had no idea what they were facing, only that whatever it was, it was now her job to deal with it. For the kids' sake, she needed to, they had no one else to depend on. All of a sudden she was forced into being everything to everybody, she just hoped she was up to it.

She kept hoping that if something could be done today, maybe they'd never even have to know. That was a pipe dream on her part, because for one thing, Kara already knew about it, so it was only fair that the boys did, too. Kate allowed herself a moment of irrational thinking because she wasn't thinking straight right now. How could she? Physically, she was managing but mentally, she was rattled.

Even if by a miracle Don was released from jail, she couldn't let him back in the house. She was too afraid now to have Don and Kara anywhere near each other. They had dodged a bullet, since Don didn't go through with his plan to hurt Kara, but Kate wasn't willing to put her daughter's safety in jeopardy by having Don back home. If Kara already had one parent she couldn't trust, then it was up to Kate to be the one she could trust. The last thing she needed now was to wonder what Don would do if he had an opportunity to be alone with Kara. She just didn't want to think about it.

The reason that he was in jail is what shattered her world. How could he even consider trying to sexually abuse their daughter? What was he thinking? For whatever the reason, and no reason would ever justify his actions, she was relieved that the act itself did not come to fruition between Don and Kara. The minute Kara started to tell Don that what he was trying to do was wrong, he stopped and thank

God for that. It was as if Kara's words snapped him back into his right mind. Kate was so thankful that's where it ended, but as far as the law was concerned, the act had been committed because there was intent on Don's part. He actually had the intent to do physical and mental harm to their sweet innocent daughter, and that is the part that Kate couldn't accept.

Kate had gotten word that Don now had a public defender. It surprised her because she thought public defenders were only for individuals who had been arrested and couldn't afford a lawyer, which they definitely could. The fact was that she refused to hire a lawyer for Don. The other fact that had bearing on the situation was that the State had said they would provide a Public Defender if Don promised to reimburse the State for the cost of his defense, since he was financially able to do so. He agreed because it was his only choice. He would have agreed to anything if they let him out.

For Kate, there was no question of what she would do, she was going to protect Kara, and if that meant hurting Don in the process, then so be it. He didn't deserve her help after all that had happened. Kate had heard of other women who stood by their husband in cases such as this, but she wasn't about to do that. How could she? How could any mother do that? She never did understand it. For Kate it wasn't even a choice. It was about her daughter and making sure she was taken care of through all of this. As far as Kate was concerned, Don could deal with the trouble he had caused on his own.

When Kate contacted the court for more information about the case, she found out that the lawyer had gotten permission to talk to Don before the arraignment, which was unusual. Apparently the lawyer had pleaded with the judge to let him see Don because of the nature of the case and the judge agreed.

The twins, Tommy and Timmy, were busy with their studies, since college was only a year away and most days, both of them stayed late at school for football practice. They were both good students, but with graduation looming, she wondered if they would each go their own way after that. Since their birth, they had done everything together and at the same time. She liked it that way and they did too. But now they were getting to the time of their lives where they each needed to make decisions about their individual futures, which Kate thought was sad, in a way. Tommy was looking at a variety of colleges and leaning toward a state college about two hours away. He was hoping for a chance to land a baseball scholarship and the state college seemed to offer the best all around package. Timmy was interested in a military career and had spoken to the Marine recruiter at his high school about all they had to offer. He was so impressed after talking to the recruiter that he rushed home that day with paperwork for Kate and Don to sign, allowing him to enlist, even though he was underage. Kate and Don said they would think about it and they told him if he still wanted to join at the time of his graduation, they would sign at that time, but not now. He was a little disappointed but then realized his parents only wanted to make sure this is really what he wanted and not something to go into half-heartedly. Kate secretly wished Timmy would go to college first and then decide what he wanted to do after that. Right now though, there was a lot more to worry about than her sons' future career choices.

The few minutes Kate had left before stepping into the shower made her thoughts drift to Kara, her only daughter, her baby. After having twin sons, Kara's birth was a pure delight. Kara was born when the twins were five years old and just as the boys were ready to start school, Kate was at home with the new baby, Kara. It was great timing and this afforded Kate the opportunity to spend the entire day with her new baby until the boys got home in the afternoon. On nice spring days, she would put Kara in the stroller and walk to the bus stop to meet the boys after school. Thinking back on those days, Kate wondered if her life would ever return to normal after today. Back then, the biggest decision she had to make all day was what to make for dinner and here she was wondering when someone would be able to get her husband out of jail. Today the biggest decision about what would happen to her family was going to be made by someone else: Judge Pearson, who was known to be fair but a real stickler for those he felt were guilty or those he felt posed a danger to the public.

The phone rang and knocked her out of the trance she was in. She jumped and leaped for the phone just to stop the noise.

"Hello?"

"Hi, this is Ken Higgins. Is Mrs. Nelson there please?"

"This is she, what can I do for you?"

"Mrs. Nelson, I wanted to call and let you know what is going on in your husband's case."

"I think I already have a good understanding of what is going on."

"You do?"

"Yes, I understand that the arraignment will take place shortly and that will be when my husband will tell the judge how he intends to plead in the case. I am sure he will say he is not guilty, but I disagree with that. I happen to believe my daughter and I will continue to do so. I also know that this is the time when the judge will let him know if he has to stay in jail or not."

"Yes, that's right."

"After what my daughter has told me you can imagine that I am not real sympathetic to his situation. Let me also tell you that from now on, I would rather you didn't call me about what is going on in my husband's case. I have the State Attorney's office keeping me informed, so it is not necessary for you to do so as well. I appreciate what you are trying to do, but please understand that I chose to side with my daughter and Don can take care of his case and how he tries to defend it by himself."

"I understand."

"In addition, if the judge does decide to let Don out of jail, please let my husband know that he is no longer welcome here because I can't take the chance of his being anywhere near my daughter."

"You do understand that the home is his as well as yours. I am not a family law attorney, but just so you understand this is not totally up to you."

"I think it is since I am the one occupying the home at the moment and I am also the one who will continue to protect my daughter, whether anyone else agrees or not. Also, I would not hesitate to file a restraining order against him and in light of what he is charged with, I don't think a judge would disagree with me. Will there be anything else, Mr. Higgins?"

"No, I think you have made everything quite clear."

"I tried to and I am glad you know where I stand. Goodbye, Mr. Higgins."

With that, Kate hung up the phone and told herself that she stood her ground and there was no way Don's lawyer could misinterpret what she said. If she could maintain that sense of composure and assuredness when it came to everything else she was going to have to face, she told herself she would be fine, but only time would tell and she really had no idea if she could or not.

CHAPTER FOUR

Don had been staring at the ceiling for so long that not only could he tell you how many tiles there were above him, but also every little mark, crack and dot on the ceiling; it was as if he had all of them etched into his mind like a mosaic. In fact, some days he would lie on the thin mattress and stare at the ceiling for so long that he could actually start to imagine he was seeing the faces of those he knew within those tiles. Those faces were blended into the lines on the ceiling and it kept him busy for hours, in addition to giving him terrible nightmares. There was nothing else to do and sometimes he even envisioned his children up there, and when he realized what he was imagining, he started to think he was going crazy. He wasn't, but the atmosphere inside the jail lent itself to things like that, and he was desperate to see the kids. He knew Kate was trying to keep them away from the situation, and he realized that might be better for them, but he missed them, no matter what else was going on. He wondered what they were thinking about all of this and what Kate had told them. He trusted that she would be honest with them, but would present it to them in a gentle way. Of course, by now she knew the reason he was arrested but he wondered if she was going to tell the kids the reason he was there. If she did decide to tell them, he hoped she would remind them of his innocence and that it was some sort of mistake and it would take time to get him out of here, but would they believe it? He hoped so, but he was worried about it. The number of worries he had now were stacking up, he could choose one and dwell on it for hours. He was fast becoming hardened to the fact he was in jail and no longer was sure he would get out in a few days, since those "few days" had already passed.

He was starting to come to grips with it, not because he had no desire to get out but because he was the only person who knew the absolute truth. So far, he had done a good job of keeping the facts to himself. What were the facts? Why was he so reluctant to tell anyone he could trust, especially Kate? For now, he figured the best defense was to stay quiet for as long as he could, to everyone. He didn't want anything he said to be taken the wrong way or to have anyone misunderstand.

Kate was siding with the police in believing that because he just "thought" of doing something with his daughter, that it was already done. But that wasn't true, so why was he being punished for something he didn't do? It made no sense. The absurdity of it all from his viewpoint was that no matter what anyone said, he was innocent. People might not like it, but that was the truth. He and Kara were the only ones who knew the truth and Kara was most likely too scared to say much of anything.

Minutes turned to hours and hours to days with time passing by at a snail's pace. There seemed to be very little movement in the case, but his lawyer warned him that's how it would be in the beginning. It was now reaching the point where it was almost unbearable for him. He longed to go back to his old life and be with his wife and kids. The really sad part of it for him was that he had a feeling they might not want him back after all this was over. It was the only thing he wanted. He learned all too quickly that he was now in a place where he couldn't talk his way out or pay his way out.

He wondered how the guys who were here for years coped with it. His time served was only a few days, but it felt so much longer than that. He couldn't imagine being in here for years at a time. He wasn't anywhere near a trial and it didn't look like his lawyer was any closer to getting him out of here. Now that the judge had denied bail, it was all so depressing because there was nothing for him to look forward to. Some of the inmates waited anxiously for visits from their family, but he also saw their indifference when no one came to visit them.

No matter what happened and for whatever length of time he had to be in jail, Don hoped he would never turn into one of those guys, the one that people forgot about once they were in jail. The one nobody seemed to care about after the visits started to become a chore. The inmate who never had visitors, received mail or had any other type of contact from the outside; he didn't want to be that guy. He prayed he wouldn't be.

Being in jail turned him into someone that he wasn't, someone he had never been before and prior to this, a person who had the respect of his family, friends and co-workers. But with that respect quickly fading from view, he felt as if everyone was slowly but surely turning against him. He usually had no visitors and Kate had no reason to come and visit him, and she wouldn't bring the kids because she didn't want to be there. He was slowly turning into a forgotten man, and that's the one thing he didn't want to be.

Don paced the area of his cell so many times it was almost as if he was a character in a 1950's movie where he was an expectant father. Pacing, constantly pacing, until he started to make himself dizzy. He had turned into the master of the "what if" scenarios. What if Kate can't forgive me for this? What if the kids don't either? What if my boss decides to fire me? What if my friends and neighbors hate me? What if I end up going crazy in here? Then, the worst question: What if I never get out of here?

The last question was the one that really bothered him. He had already been denied bail and the emergency motion filed by his lawyer had been denied, so here he sat. His chances of getting out of jail anytime soon were slim to none. The real question was what people might really think of him when, and if, he did get out of jail. Not only would he be surrounded by the stigma of having been in jail, but what about when they heard what he had been charged with? He knew that if an innocent person was charged with a horrendous crime, no matter what the outcome, it would scar him and put a black mark on him for the rest of his life. If he was found not guilty, the stigma of all this would be hard to get rid of and he would forever be known as someone who tried to molest his daughter, even if it wasn't true. Either way, he was done for.

Kate's life was teetering between the life she knew and one she might not want to know. All she wanted to do was curl up in her bed, cry and somehow, make the world go away. Slowly, Kate climbed the stairs and headed into her bedroom. The bright Florida sunlight filtered its way through the sheer floor length draperies as she sighed and sat down on the bed, thinking, always thinking. Her body was tired and craved relief, but so was her mind. She was tired of thinking about Don all the time and what was going to happen to all of them. She knew if Don had to stay in jail for any length of time, everything was going to fall on her. She'd accept it because she loved her kids and would do what she had to do. But that didn't mean it was going to be easy, and it didn't mean she was going to like it.

She stretched out and pulled the covers nearly over her head. She'd made a little cocoon for herself in that room, feeling like she had blocked out everyone from coming near her. She'd wished she could do that on a larger scale so that no one could invade her safe little world, the one she used to have. She needed to realize that there was no more safe little world for her. That was gone now, and had gone fast. As she put her head down, she felt the warm tears run down her cheek and hit the pillow. She lay there and tried to imagine the enormity of it all, as she willed the tears to go away, but they refused.

The crying session would be the first of many, and after the tears stopped, Kate still wouldn't know how she was going to deal with it all. She had absolutely no clue and that's what scared her the most.

CHAPTER FIVE

A few hours later, Kate opened her eyes and realized her life as she knew it was about to change. Feelings of uncertainty about everything in her life were popping in and out of her head. Her mind was in a total state of upheaval. She couldn't be sure of anything now. She was used to being the one in control, the one who had a handle on everything, the one the kids came to most often because she was the one with the answers, the one who ran all aspects of their lives. Kate had let Don think otherwise and that was OK with her. If he wanted to think that it was him who managed it all, it didn't bother her, because that was a small price to pay when she knew all the time that things were just the opposite. Kate was the one who "didn't sweat the small stuff" but she had suddenly been thrown into a world she wanted no part of; one where things were going to be difficult, frustrating and most of all, heartbreaking. She knew all that was coming, she just had to brace herself for it. She started to eerily think of what life might be like weeks from now, once people got to know what was going on and what they would say when they did. People could be so mean, even when they didn't know the whole story. She shuddered at the thought of it. This was going to be a nightmare for all of them and she had to be strong for herself and the kids; she was all they had now and she was desperately afraid of their reaction when they found out. Obviously, the only one who wasn't going to be surprised was Kara; she was the one who was the true victim and Kate vowed then and there to stand behind her daughter, who she loved more than anything or anyone in this world, aside from her sons. When it came down to making a choice between her husband and her kids, there really was no choice; it was the kids. It would kill her if that was what this was going to come down to, but she would deal with it. Kate was a strong woman, and no matter how this turned out, she and the kids would survive it. Her only problem now was convincing herself of it. She was determined to be there for the kids through all of this; especially Kara, her daughter, her baby, her most precious. Her feelings for Don would remain to be seen; no one could predict the future. She knew she had been a good wife to him, but if someone hurt him or her kids, she was like an angered tigress. This situation was like no other she had to deal with before, it was her feelings for her husband versus her feelings for her daughter; and her love for her daughter could never be shaken. Her love for her husband could change; especially if he really was guilty of this disgusting charge. All Kate could think of was that if it was proven that Don was guilty, and God help him if he was, she would see to it that he suffered. It was totally out of character for her to wish something like that on anyone; most of all her husband. But being asked to deal with this situation, and she was only at the start of it, could prove to be beyond difficult. The hard part was going to occur when she had to keep the kids away from it as much as possible. Once the news "broke" and everyone got wind of what was going on, it would be impossible to shield anyone from it, especially the kids. She worried about the reactions of friends and family, the effect it might have on her job and on her own psyche; which was the most fragile of all. That was the one thing that would take the most time to repair and that wouldn't be easy.

Don knew he was just biding his time till the trial, but that wasn't scheduled for quite a few months. He worried that being in jail would add to his problems at home: his relationship with Kate and the kids, family finances, and having people find out about all of this. He hated the idea of people being shocked about the situation without his getting a chance to have his say. When people heard about it, they would just assume he was guilty. That's how it was with stuff like this: no one ever listened to the whole story; they jumped to conclusions first without taking the time to hear all the details. It bothered him that people would get the wrong idea about what happened. He had no control over the situation, no control of working on getting out of jail and that's the part he hated; he was at everyone else's mercy and the feeling of helplessness was starting to weigh on him.

For the first few days he was here, the jail was just as unbearable then as it was now, the only difference being that back then, he was optimistic about getting out. Now all that had faded, knowledge that he was going to be here for awhile had finally sunk in. He wasn't going anywhere anytime soon. He knew that the same dirty gray walls he was surrounded by each day were the first things he would wake up to each morning. They were the same walls he looked at throughout the day and the last things he saw at night. Anyone who could be described as a "creature of habit" would love this place because nothing ever changed. Even the correctional officers started to look the same after awhile. That's because they all had the same attitude toward the inmates and they had a job to do, which didn't include being friendly. That attitude should have been reserved for the other guys, the ones who had a rap sheet as long as your arm, the ones who had made a career out of being in jail. He had no intention of being part of that group and would do anything he could to avoid it. He just wanted out, it didn't matter if he had to pay thousands of dollars or abide by whatever terms the court set. He would agree to any kind of plea offer, his only goal right now was to get out of there, no matter what it took.

Kate would be supportive of whatever the terms were because he was thinking all she wanted was to have him at home, too. He was wrong; Kate wanted what was right. She wasn't about to have her husband be charged with sexual battery on a child, his own child, and then just politely welcome him back into their home, like he was away on vacation or a business trip. No way, he needed to pay for what he did, or tried to do, and if the jail didn't want to prolong his sentence, fine. But Kate knew that she had her own punishment in mind for him. As far as she was concerned, he was never coming back to their house. It was ridiculous to think that he could, after all that had happened. Did he really think that getting out of jail would absolve him of everything he had done and that his old life was available to him just for the taking? He would have been surprised to learn how she really did feel. Up till now, on the rare occasions when she did see him, that's the one thing they never talked bout. Each of them wanted to bring it up, but for now, that subject was taboo. Neither of them was ready to discuss it, and they didn't know if they could accept what they would hear. Each of them was afraid to bring it up to the other, fearing the worst of their thoughts coming out, starting a fight they couldn't finish. Kate felt an ongoing rage when she thought of what he did, or tried to do (she wasn't sure yet which one it was) to their daughter, and what more he might have wanted to do before he got caught. Kate hated what all of them were forced to go through now because of Don's bad decision. She was thankful, sort of, that she found out about it now, what if this sordid thing had dragged on and on?

At the same time, he was her husband, but that fact alone didn't warrant loyalty. It warranted thinking, a lot of it. She was the one who had the burden of trying to deal with all of this. Each one of them were victims, and Kate knew that the situation was going to negatively affect the kids, and she hated that for them. She couldn't change what had happened to them and she knew that all of them would be traumatized to some degree. She understood that feelings could not be dictated, only felt from the heart. Kate couldn't tell the kids how to feel, they would end up deciding that for themselves. However the kids thought of their dad from now on was up to them. She wouldn't take that away from them. She knew it was going to be hard on them and equally as hard on her seeing them in such pain. She was now in the company of millions of other mothers who tried to take away the misery from their children. Kate knew she was powerless to do so, which added to her frustration, but that wouldn't stop her from trying.

There was one bright spot on today's agenda for Don: he had been told that Kate scheduled a visit this afternoon, so at least he had something to look forward to. That fact alone would make the morning bearable. He had wanted to tell her things that were burdening him, the things that were weighing on his heart, but it never seemed the right time to bring it up. He wanted to apologize to her for the situation he had put her in. All of a sudden, she was left alone to handle everything: kids, job, household and just her own feelings at Don being in jail and why he was there. It was a lot to take on and he knew she was a strong woman, but this was a lot to ask of anyone. He worried she might turn against him over all of this, and even though he had been with her for many years, sometimes it was hard to read her. She could be mysterious at times, and it was impossible to know what she was thinking. He worried that she would turn the kids against him, but decided she wasn't a vindictive person and no matter what, he was their father, in jail or not. His "model father" status was gone — and he didn't know if he could ever get it back after this. He was the same person he had always been and would not treat the kids any differently now. The real question was if the kids would go on to accept love from him. That nagged at him all the time, and he worried more about it than what was going to ultimately happen to him. He couldn't eat, couldn't sleep, and with the worry he carried on his shoulders, it all played out in the form of his getting run down physically. Whenever Kate saw him, he looked tired. She commented on that fact and he asked her to understand for a minute what it must be like for him to be separated from her, the kids and the house they all shared. He knew her motive in saying it was sincere, but that didn't change the fact that he was in jail on a serious charge and pretending it was anything different was futile.

Don asked about the kids at his every meeting with Kate and she would tell him about their school activities and the sports they participated in. But what he really wanted to know was how they were doing mentally, how all of this was affecting them. He understood she was trying to keep life normal for them and they both agreed that was the way to handle it. He wanted to know what they were thinking about all of this and how they were coping. By now, he knew the word of his being there was starting to leak out and hoped his kids didn't have to suffer on his account. The twins were nearly grown and were physically able to handle themselves. They were both on the high school football team and were in good physical shape. Don felt they had the strength and muscle to take care of anything that came their way. But Kara was the delicate flower; she was the one who didn't have the protection of her older brothers when she was at school. Kate had made arrangements to work only half days and made sure she picked Kara up from school each day so as to lessen the time she might have to suffer any type of ridicule from her classmates. Kate tried to limit the time Kara would be alone with the other kids at school. So now, Kate added another task to her daily routine: part-time bodyguard. Her daughter was her priority; she didn't mind, but it was tiring and would be so much easier if she could just allow Kara to ride the bus, like the other kids did. But Kara was in a different situation now and she had to be protected; after all, she was still a child. She was her own one woman carpool. If this had been a different time of the year, she could have gotten some help with the twins and had them pick up Kara after school. They were busy each afternoon with football practice, so there was no time for them to help Kate. So for now, Kate drove Kara to school each morning, went on to work and picked Kara up each afternoon.

She was trying to let them continue with the schedule they kept before Don was arrested and so far it was working well. She knew all this was temporary and that things were going to get more complicated in Don's case. She decided to leave well enough alone until something happened to change it all, which might be any day now. Lately, it seemed just when things were going along OK and were on an even keel, someone or something threw a monkey wrench into the mix and then it was up to Kate to make the adjustments for all of them. Maybe in her next life, she would be a victim's advocate. By then, she would have had plenty of practice.

CHAPTER SIX

This morning Kate's visit to Don was being done out of a half-hearted gesture, not one of any pure desire to see him. What he had done to their family was unforgivable and she was a strong support system for the kids; especially Kara. It took her awhile to get to the place she was now but she felt it was the right way to go. She couldn't stand idly by and be the dutiful supportive wife after what he had done to their daughter; that part of their personal relationship was over. There was absolutely no question that Don was a disgrace to all of them.

She was extremely embarrassed when people stared at her while she did routine tasks. She could only imagine what they were think-ing and saying about her now that the news about Don was starting to get around. In a matter of months, they had gone from the All-American nuclear family to a one with someone in jail, putting an invisible black mark on all of them; she couldn't see it, or feel it, but it was definitely there. It was amazing how fast the family had lost their status and how people they knew were now starting to snub them. Kate felt if they knew the whole story they would most likely feel sorry for her and the kids, but there was no use trying to explain the long sad story to everyone. Why bother? It was so disgusting even to Kate, that she felt uncomfortable having to repeat it to anyone. If she explained it once, she would have to do it a thousand times. Even so, people were going to think what they wanted to anyway, so let them. Kate knew the truth, and that's all that mattered. If they wanted to think bad about her and the kids because of something that Don did, then that was their choice. She couldn't spend every minute of her time worrying about what other people were thinking. If she did, she wouldn't have time for anything else. It had been a long, grueling decision and even though it was hard for her to come to terms with it at times, she knew it was the right one for herself and her family. Kate found herself spending many afternoons alone so she could try to concentrate on the situation with no outside distractions. It was a thought process that required a lot of peace and quiet, which she seemed to have an abundance of these days. Her mornings were filled with taking Kara to school and then going on to the realty company she worked for. She was grateful that her boss had let her adjust her working hours to mornings only. Sometimes she had to meet with a potential buyer in the afternoon, but that was rare. Most of her afternoons were free and she spent them in deep thought concerning her feelings for Don and how she was going to manage the family on her own – long term. Kate had been thrown into a world of split second changes and heart wrenching decisions and so far, she was balancing them fairly well.

The time to make a decision and actually stick with it was now. After so much time devoted to their particular lifestyle, she was resigned to the fact that her life with Don and the kids would be changed forever; never to be the same as what she had experienced with them for the past eighteen years. She was trying to accept it, but after eighteen years, it was hard to start all over. She loved her former life. It was one that made her grateful for having the best of both worlds: her working life and her home life. Like the old saying, "When things sound too good to be true", that's when you need to re-evaluate because a change is coming, and not always one for the better.

Kate continued to visit Don in jail, but not as much as she used to when he first was arrested. For one thing, back then, she thought he wouldn't be there long; he would be out in a matter of days and most importantly, she was sure of his innocence. But now that it looked like he might be facing a longer stay, she wasn't quite as anxious to visit. As soon as she saw the familiar sign, "Preston County Jail" it immediately gave her goose bumps. She'd start to break out in a cold sweat, her hands would all of a sudden go icy on her and she felt like she was on display. It was a place and an atmosphere she didn't belong in and the other people there made her uncomfortable, too. She herself started to feel like a common criminal just being in the waiting room. Women there saw her as "one of them" but she told herself she was different; she didn't belong here. After she gave it some thought, she realized she did belong here, whether she liked to admit it or not. Her husband was in jail, so that fact alone made her belong. She could deny it all she wanted to and try to hide it, but the fact remained she had earned a place in the "wife with a husband in jail" club and she was in it for the long haul. She was slowly getting used to the fact that she was required to register at the information desk when she got there. She was the one who had to sit in the waiting area and try not to focus on those around her. It was funny because when you try to act inconspicuous, it never works, then you "overcorrect" and you appear even more noticeable. She would see some of the same women on the rare occasions when she did visit. Most of the time, she would visit to ask Don something about the kids, the bills or the house. Her visits weren't personal and she made that fact clear to him so there was no misunderstanding. Some of the women she waited with smiled at her, like the young woman who always sat in the corner and never said a word to anyone, except whisper to the toddler in her lap. Kate did notice when they called this woman by name, she handed off the toddler to the woman with her, as she followed the jail employee. Kate felt sorry for her, and for the rest of them who were here to visit a loved one. It was tough on the ones who were left behind to pick up the pieces of their lives, without the love and support of the person being held here. Then Kate noticed a nicely dressed man about Don's age and he too, smiled at her. She was surprised to hear him speak to her, as he sipped hot coffee from a paper cup.

"You look like you could use a cup of coffee. Can I get one for you?"

"Oh, no, thanks for asking though."

"You're welcome. I'm here to see my son."

Kate all of a sudden was at a loss for words, she couldn't very well answer with "Oh, that's nice." So instead, she answered with, "Well, I'm here visiting a family member, too."

That's all Kate wanted to tell him. She always got a little uneasy when people she didn't know were a little too nosy. Kate didn't know this guy from Adam and she wasn't about to divulge any information about herself. For all she knew, the guy could be an ex-con trying to see if she lived alone, etc. Kate had learned to keep her guard up, especially now.

"It's not easy, is it?"

"No, it isn't. It's terrible, actually."

In between the conversation, Kate tried to size the guy up. He looked respectable, but not enough for Kate to want to take it much further. He was probably lonely, like her. Maybe he meant no harm, she wasn't sure. She just wanted him to go away and leave her alone.

"I know what you mean. My son got involved with the wrong type of people at the wrong time and now here he sits. I'll just be glad when it's over. Thankfully, it should only be another few months."

"That's great. I am just starting with this, so I hope I can take it."

"You'll do fine."

The woman at the desk called the next name on the list, and thankfully, it was the guy Kate was talking to. She wanted to get rid of him and now she didn't have to think of a way to pull it off. Making small talk wasn't something Kate delighted in and especially with someone she didn't know or want to know. Kate was the type of person who took no pleasure in chit chat with strangers. In fact, she always wondered why people in doctors' waiting rooms always felt the need to talk to others around them. She had never had any interest in it, and that lack of interest was especially heightened now. It was the last thing she needed. She had enough problems without adding talking to a guy who had a son in jail. Kate wasn't some lost waif on a city street corner, she could fend for herself, without the polite small talk.

Kate always felt slightly intimidated whenever she visited Don. That's because she felt like she was being treated like a child on each visit, since she had to follow a jail employee and be escorted to the place where Don was brought out to her. She was a grown woman and even though she understood the need for the procedures that had to be followed, she didn't like it. That was another reason why she debated over having the kids there too much. It was too degrading for them to see their father in a place like this and she really didn't want them to have to experience it. She desperately tried to keep them from the jail, but every now and then they expressed an interest in seeing Don. She explained to them that there was a lot of stuff going on at the beginning of his case and when things calmed down a little, there would be plenty of time to visit and spend some time with him. That answer seemed to satisfy them, at least for the moment. She knew they would ask her about seeing him later on, but that was then, and this was now. In fact, that's how her life was now; a series of things that had to be dealt with in a timely manner. The things that could wait, did. The things that couldn't wait were dealt with now. It was the story of her new life and the way it worked. She didn't have to like it, she just had to accept it and make sure it got done.

Her visits to Don were starting to feel forced and it was almost as if they were turning into a chore, not a desire. Even though he was always glad to see her, after awhile they started to run out of things to say to each other and she knew that's when they were headed for trouble. Kate's feelings of doubt towards him were mounting and she managed to keep them in check up till now. Recently she found her feelings toward him changing and she was unsure how to manage them.

Kate now found herself going to the jail less and less. Her friends told her she was crazy because according to them, she owed him nothing. Still, she was trying to do what she thought was right. Kara would be protected no matter what and that is the time she would feel no loyalty to Don. The jail visits to Don were becoming a chore, not something she looked forward to. There was an ever growing lull in conversation between them and the gaps between their words were getting ever larger. Kate worried that Don would sense her uneasiness about their relationship, but so far he hadn't said anything about it. Their conversations were no longer like they used to be when he was at home. That's because back then he would have news of his day and what happened at work to tell her about. She, in turn, would be able to tell him about the realty work she did and how the day went with the kids. During these visits, there was nothing new he could tell her from the day before. Life in the jail was the same every day, nothing ever changed there, so what could possibly be new for him? He depended on her to bring him the news. Kate would usually visit him after she got off work, while the kids were still in school. That way, she didn't have to drag them down there and they were too busy with school activities to go anyway. At least Don was understanding about that and said he would rather their concentration be on school right now, not him. Kate did appreciate hearing that from him and she had no intention of bringing the kids there if she didn't have to. He said he understood, but she wondered if he did and was only saying it, but not really meaning it. At this point Kate didn't care what Don thought about it. She had decided that it was now her job alone to protect her children, and if that included keeping them away from their own father, then so be it, at least for now. If and when he demanded to see them is when she would start to worry about it.

Coming to the jail sporadically was both depressing and embarrassing. Each time she came to visit, she had to spend time in the waiting area until they directed her to where he was. This was the part of the visit she hated most. Usually she was too nervous to spend the time reading or browsing through a magazine. She would look at the other women surrounding her and their cold hard looks and watery eyes gave way to how sad they were. You could tell that by just looking at them and Kate didn't dare talk to any of them, they all seemed mad at the world. The last thing she needed right now was to hear anyone else's hard luck story; she had her own to deal with. They all looked like they realized what was happening, but weren't sure how to fix it. Who did? If she was so smart, she wouldn't be sitting here either.

Right then, Kate came to an empowering decision. This would be one of her very last visits to the jail. No longer would she put herself in a place where she felt this uncomfortable.

She had no obligation to visit Don, she was only doing it because she thought she had to, or at least that she should. When she finally realized it was her choice whether to visit Don or not, she chose not to. She owed him nothing and now it was her turn to make all the rules. She liked playing the game that way, and she intended to win.

CHAPTER SEVEN

Things finally started to settle into a routine for Kate and the kids. She didn't take them to see Don that much; there was really no point considering her feelings on the whole thing. Actually, after having all this time to think about the situation, she really wasn't all that enthused about doing much of anything for or with him, which included her own visits to him, which were starting to dwindle in frequency. Kate was surprised how her feelings for Don had changed and how the feelings just happened in a logical progression, with no serious intent on her part. Previous to this, she had worried about it constantly, but now the whole issue seemed like it was going to resolve itself. She didn't plan it; it just happened. Kate had wrestled with the question of her feelings for Don, or lack thereof, for a long time now and she was finally able to tell herself that what she was feeling was right. It was almost as if it was nature's quirky way of taking care of things. She knew if she put her mind to it, the answers would come to her and they did. Kate told herself that she would accept what her mind told her and despite any fleeting moments of being unsure about them, her feelings were genuine and here to stay.

The kids were at the point now where they were mostly stoic about Don being in jail and Don in general. They were learning to live without him and they were adjusting well. She was proud of them, for what they had been through already and how they were handling it. What troubled Kate was what they still had to go through and she hoped she and the kids had enough stamina and strength to muster it all. They had done just fine so far but the thing is that Don's case was going to get worse before it got better. Kate knew it and she imagined the kids knew it too but none of them dared mention it. It was the old "out of sight, out of mind" thing and if that's what they needed to get to the end of each day, then so be it. Kate wasn't happy with any of what they had to currently deal with, it was just safe to say that she was "settled" with it. There was too much to think about if she let her mind wander, so she tried not to; it helped keep in check the little sanity she had left. She was acting like the brain police: don't let them think about what was going on and they wouldn't have to deal with it. Contradictory thought invaded her every move but for now she had to keep things as normal as she could, for the sake of the kids and it was doing her some good, too.

Just the physical part of actually going to the jail was getting old and she wasn't enthused about seeing Don any longer. She was doing what was expected of her as his wife in that she was trying to handle things at home, but beyond that, she just wasn't happy about doing much for him. She knew she couldn't go on the way she had been and it was time to set some new boundaries. Now that the state attorney and his staff had taken over the case on Kara's behalf, she didn't have to have any personal dealings with Don's attorney. She decided she needed a break and she went to the kitchen and poured herself a tall glass of lemonade and went outside on the back deck to soak up some Florida sunshine. Kate stretched out on the chaise lounge and never really realized what a simple little pleasure it was to be out here enjoying the fresh air and nobody reminding her of all the bad stuff in her life at the moment, she could do that herself. It was the few minutes of peace she desperately needed. The neighborhood was still quiet because the kids weren't home from school yet and everything was still. There were no roaring car engines, no emergency vehicle sirens, no screaming babies or loud neighborhood children to contend with and she was grateful for the silence.

This would be the first time she actually got to be outside and start on this year's tan. The warmth felt comforting to her and added to her resolve to keep up with things she would normally do. She didn't show her age and she was still attractive by anyone's standards. Men would always give her a second look but she wondered what they would think if they knew she was married to a pedophile and that he was in jail. Of course, Don hadn't been convicted yet, but just to be accused of such a thing was the same thing to her as being found guilty. If Don had been accused of another type of crime, Kate would have been adamant about his innocence, because she would have never believed he was capable of doing anything like that. But then again, she never thought he would try to hurt Kara for his own pleasure, either. It bothered her that after being with him for this long, maybe she didn't know him at all, which came at her like a swift kick in the stomach. She knew that she could not give him her full support and with Kara not admitting to it yet, but not denying it either, Kate knew they were in trouble. She knew her daughter and she felt Kara would tell her everything that went on when she was ready. The last thing Kara needed now was to be reminded of the whole terrible ordeal and be forced to think about it. The poor kid was being tormented just knowing what she had experienced with her own father. It was so disgusting to Kate that at times she felt she wanted to run to the jail and beat the hell out of him. Yet, she thought it might be better if she could just keep her cool and let Don sweat it out. Let him think none of them cared, and even though that was getting closer to the truth each day, Kate knew not getting visits from the family would be the worst punishment of all. So she opted for that and was happy with it. If friends or relatives called to see how she was doing, she would tell them she hadn't seen Don in awhile, that she just couldn't do it. What was closer to the truth was the fact that she knew it was eating away at him, not seeing her or the kids that often. It was her own way of getting back at him and she loved it. It made her look like the weak one, but she didn't mind being weak if it meant Don was getting a taste of his own medicine and she was secretly glad. It was working and getting the effect she wanted and no one was the wiser. The situation was turning out just the way she wanted it to and she couldn't be happier. It was the perfect solution to allow her to keep going, have Don suffer and have her and the kids start to make a life for themselves without him. The preliminary pieces were starting to fall into place and all she had to do was let it happen. It was the perfect plan and happening all on its' own.

Kate was knee deep in satisfying thought when the relaxing silence was broken with the shrill ringing of the telephone.

She got to her feet and headed to the kitchen counter and picked up the receiver. "Hello, Nelson residence". Kate started to answer the phone this way lately because she could never be sure who would be calling. All kinds of women's groups had started to contact her and most of the time she wasn't in the mood to listen to what they had to say. They would try to convince her stand her ground with Don and all she would ever tell them is that she intended to stand behind her daughter throughout all of this. She appreciated the gesture, but she was trying to deal with all of this on her own. Anyway, did these callers really think she would abandon her daughter now? No way!

Kate soon came to realize that being a victim (or a victim's mother) was a job in itself. All of a sudden, her mailbox was flooded with paperwork and it was hard just keeping up with it all and most of the time she would just make a big pile of envelopes on her desk. She knew that at some time soon she would have to deal with it, but not yet, she needed that one last resolve to tackle the pile and she wasn't ready. She hoped that someday she would have the strength to deal with it all, but this was all so new and shocking that she needed more time to let it sink in, let it get into her whole being that this is what her life now was, being the wife of an inmate, and at the same time, being the mother of the victim.

Her motherly instincts were on call and she felt the claws coming out when it came to anything dealing with Kara. She refused to let herself or her daughter become more of a victim. Don would just have to suffer the consequences as she watched from the sidelines. She was adamant about Don being made to suffer for what he had done.

How could anyone be expected to visit someone in jail, whether it be your spouse or not, after his being accused of sexual battery on a child under 12? The whole thing was beyond the point of embarrassment for her. Even though she wasn't the one there, the fact that she was close to someone who was made her an automatic target for gossip. She tried to ignore it but sometimes it was hard not to notice those around her who started whispering when she approached. She could only imagine what they were saying. Kate knew the best way to handle it was to ignore them, but sometimes it was so frustrating that she just wanted to yell, "HEY! I'm not the guilty one here! I just happen to be married to the one who is!" Plus, the situation was especially sticky since her own daughter was the victim. Yet, Kate knew it was now up to her to handle the kids and their emotions, as much as she could. She saw no reason to visibly upset them by taking them to the jail and being mortified that their own father was locked up. It was just too sad for her to watch.

Even with visits to the jail, it was still hard for Kate to imagine their previous life as a family was now gone forever. It was almost as if a bad dream was coming true. That bad dream was unfolding before her eyes and she couldn't wake up to make it go away. It was a slow churning in the pit of her stomach alternating with the headache she had just from the realization of it all.

"Life is so fragile" is the cliché she had heard for years, but never paid all that much attention to it. She was starting to understand more fully what that statement meant.

So Kate's world had now evolved into a phase where she could finally admit to herself and to the world around her how much she despised what Don had done and because of it, her feelings for him were being challenged at every turn. She was finished playing the little wife left at home to pick up the pieces. Now she was the new Kate, the strong one. The one who would stand up for herself and the kids, the one who wasn't going to do everything Don told her to do unless she herself thought it was a good idea and the one who was not going to let the words or reactions of others put down her kids or herself. She was ready to take on whatever came up and she knew she had the support of the kids and her sister, Lori. As long as she had that, she didn't need anyone else, including Don. He had put himself there and now he was on his own to try and deal with it. Kate was taking a hard line on her feelings about Don but she had to, to keep her sanity and her peace of mind. What kind of mother would she be if she felt that Don was still the loving husband and father he always had been?

She'd read about cases where a daughter had been sexually abused only to find out that the mother either didn't believe the child or stuck by the husband, even though it was obvious that he was not telling the truth. How could any mother side with her husband in that situation? She felt sorry for the girls who had moms like that. What a tragic thing for them to have to live through. Silently, Kate cursed all the mothers like that, the ones who were so desperate to have a man that they were willing to sacrifice the well-being of their daughters in the process.

She knew now that Don was no longer the man he was before and she had no choice but to come to terms with it. Kate believed at first that this whole thing was a classic case of mistaken identity because Don had planted that idea in her head and she bought it, at first. When she found out the truth that he was guilty, she had to re-alize what took place and deal with it for what it was. How could she let herself be sucked into believing that what he told her was actually the truth? She was beginning to have doubts about a lot of the things he had told her recently and she hated being in a position like that. Kate was strong enough to know the difference between the truth and the story Don had cooked up to make himself look good.

Things had taken a dramatic turn in their household. She wouldn't have to pretend she had feelings for Don any longer. At least she could be herself in front of the kids and she knew that in years to come, they would respect her for it. In fact, the more she thought about it, the more she respected herself. Her motherly instincts to protect her kids against everything connected with Don were obvious. After many weeks of having to hide her true feelings, she could finally let her hair down. Up till now, she was not only trying to shield her children from the situation, but in doing that, she ended up shielding herself, too. The time for that was gone; it was time to face Don's situation and what was happening with him. It wasn't good, but there was some sort of satisfaction in knowing she didn't have to hide it anymore. She knew that in the worst case, if Don had to stay in jail for an extended period of time, she would have to take responsibility for everything at home. Up till now, she was taking charge of it all, but found herself doing it without full permission. It was as if the spirit within her was fighting it. But now that she was convinced her feelings for Don had changed, she was more at ease with her transition to being the parent to shoulder all the responsibility, not just some of it.

Her new role gave her a chance to see just what she was made of; she was of good Irish and German stock and this was her time to shine for the kids and for herself. If her parents had been alive, she knew they would have fought for her and the kids, tooth and nail. This wasn't the time for pity, from them or anyone else, it was the time to pull herself up by her bootstraps and show the world what she was made of. She could do it, she would do it. World, watch out, here comes Kate Nelson, the woman who will fight like a tiger to protect her kids and fight the system if they have any ideas of releasing Don anytime soon.

Her mission would be his punishment and knowing he could never make up for what he did to their daughter, or maybe what he tried to do, she wasn't sure. That's the part she didn't want to think about. Either way, she would see that justice prevailed, even if it took her whole lifetime to see it happen. She decided right then and there that if the court system wouldn't do it, she would do it herself. What was that saying? "Hell hath no fury like a woman scorned?" That statement applied to mothers, too.

CHAPTER EIGHT

The weeks since Don's arrest had not only taken a toll on Kate, but now the kids were starting to feel the pressure. No matter how Kate tried to shield them, she found out all too quickly how mean and vicious people could be, even those you thought were your friends.

Up till now, the twins took the bus to school each day, but as the days passed, Kate knew she had to make other arrangements. The kids on the bus had started to taunt the twins with sayings like, "Make room for jail boy", or "Step aside, let Jail Daddy through", and some were much more graphic and vulgar than that. The boys assured her they could handle it but were not disappointed when she suggested maybe they should look at buying a used car for them to share and take to school. Of course, she realized once they got to school, they would have the same problem, but at least she could shield them on the way to school. Once they got there, there wasn't much she could do. This was their senior year and taking them out of that school was out of the question.

The boys were in good physical shape and although she didn't want them getting into fights over the fact that their dad was in jail, she knew if they were faced with a situation where they had to defend themselves, they could do it. Besides, she told them the old "safety in numbers" rule was very true and others were less likely to start something with either of them as long as they were together. Kate wasn't sure if they bought it, but it was worth a try. She wasn't telling them to start a fight with anyone, but deep down, she would not be disappointed if they stood up for themselves and came to blows with someone who deserved it. Unfortunately, sometimes using force was the only way to get the attention of someone with a mouth that was too big for his own good.

On the other hand, Kara seemed to be doing OK and wasn't having any of the ridicule from her classmates that the boys were. In Kara's circle, it seemed like only a few of the kids knew her dad was in jail, and of those, they probably didn't know why. They were still young and Kate hoped the parents of those kids had some sense of decency to want to protect their children by not telling them all the details of the arrest and why it happened in the first place.

There are some things that are better left unsaid. Of course, Kate always had her guard up because she was aware just how vulnerable Kara was to any kind of crude comment. It was a difficult position for Kate to be in because not only did she feel betrayed as the mother of the victim, but as a wife at the same time.

It wasn't a snub against Kara, it was more like just feeling bad because if there was such a thing as a "second" victim, she was it, and she knew it, she felt it. All the while she was trying to protect Kara, she was acutely aware of the fact that the only protection all of them had was her. On a good day, she could recite the words of Helen Reddy's "I Am Woman" verbatim and feel as if she could conquer the world. On other days, she felt as if it was her against the world, and she was on the losing side. Sometimes she felt so very alone in all of this and she longed to be in that "take me away" commercial. She knew that running away from a problem never solved anything, but it sure was tempting. So many days she would dream about it, about just taking the kids to someplace far off where nobody would find them, and never come back. It would be so easy to do, but she couldn't take the kids away from everything and everyone they knew, that wouldn't be fair. If this only affected her, she might have considered it. She would've let the chips fall where they may. She would've also let Don fend for himself and she would have gotten herself out of the picture a long time ago. Being the wife of a guy arrested on sexual battery on a child wasn't the most pleasant thing to think about. If they threw the book at Don so be it, it wasn't her worry, it wasn't like she cared. It was more like let's get this over with, I'm tired of it already, but that wasn't about to happen anytime soon. Closer to the truth was that this mess had just gotten started and the end of it was a long way off. She constantly wondered if they would survive it all, she and the kids, but only time would tell. It seemed as if time was all they had because the whole process was crawling along at a snail's pace. So many days she wondered if it would ever end. Whenever that day was destined to be, she would be ready for it. The hard thing for her to face right now was that this thing was long from over.

Kate jumped at the shrill ring of the phone. She answered hesitantly because she never knew if it was a crank call. She had recently found out that there were some really sick people in this world and unfortunately, some of them liked to harass people when they were in the midst of a crisis. So Kate made it a rule that she was the only one to answer the house phone. This way, if it was a crank call, she could handle it without having the kids get upset, they had enough to deal with. The call was from someone asking her if she wanted to subscribe to the local paper.

"No, I don't want to subscribe to the paper! If I did, I would call you, not the other way around!" Seeing the paper in front of her every day was the last thing she needed. As if she wanted to be reminded of what was happening with Don! The newspaper had taken the liberty to include every little detail of the case and put it out there for all to see.

She knew they had a job to do, but that didn't mean she had to like it. They never made mention of Kara by name, due to the fact that she was a minor. But if people knew that Don had been arrested on the charge and they knew who his daughter was, it was like yelling it through a megaphone; newspapers did not advocate privacy, only sales.

Kate was at the point where she had enough of people trying to hound her for details and some of the people asked her things that were just downright rude and none of their business. She was starting to lose her temper, which was totally out of character for her. She was turning into a person even she didn't like, but the stress of it all was making her that way. What she really needed was to get away from it all, but this wasn't the time to be thinking about that. There was just too much going on. The kids needed her now more than ever and she had to keep her strength up in order to protect them. Ever since Don was arrested, she turned into their shield, but the problem was that there was no shield for her. Lori would have been glad to take over that role, but Kate wanted to handle things on her own. Each time she was either able to prevent a crisis or diffuse one, it was a feather in her cap. She held her head high with satisfaction and told herself she no longer needed protection from Don, she was extremely capable of handling her own affairs – and Don's criminal charges. As Kate thumbed through the day's mail, she noticed a letter addressed to her from the local radio station. It read:

Dear Ms. Nelson:

We are aware of the recent arrest of your husband on a sexual battery with a minor charge. In the next few weeks, we are featuring that very subject as one of our topics during our pre-recorded daytime talk show. The show airs at 12:00 each day, following the "Noonday News".

In light of the recent developments concerning your husband's case, you would certainly make a most interesting addition to the show. Please call our office at the number below and let us know if you would like to join our panel of distinguished guests........

Kate's initial reaction to the letter was to say no, definitely not. Right after all of this happened, Kate was trying to keep the whole thing quiet, but eventually the "news" got out and then she had absolutely no control of who knew about it and who didn't. So why should Kate even consider doing it when she wanted the least amount of people as possible to be aware of what was happening with Don? Kate discussed it with her sister, who said that it might be a way for Kate to finally "clear the air" of how she was feeling. Her sister Lori thought it might be therapeutic for her, but Kate wasn't so sure. Did the old saying, "Misery loves company" fit here? Kate thought it might be both educational for those viewing a show such as this, as well as give her a chance to tell her story to the local community. She could finally tell her story, with all the facts that she knew up to this point. So many people had the wrong idea of what happened and it would be her one chance to set the record straight. She decided to think about it for a few days, but she couldn't wait too long because she was sure the TV station wanted an answer as soon as they could get one.

"So why do you have to be on a show and talk about it for?" Tim was at a loss as to why his mother would even consider doing something like that. He couldn't understand it.

"It would be a chance for me to set the record straight – to explain what really happened. I am so tired of hearing about what people think they know."

"But everyone already knows what happened! Why do you have to say it all over again?"

"It's not about saying it all over again. It's about saying what really did happen, how our family is coping and how we are going to come out of this in one piece. Plus, it might be a help to someone else going through it right now, too. Suppose there is a young girl around Kara's age watching the show and she is being abused. Just from watching the show she might have the strength to tell someone and get some help. That fact alone makes me think I want to do it. Sometimes when you are in a rough situation, just seeing someone in the same boat can really help and that's what I'm thinking about."

"OK, but it's not your job to save the world all by yourself."

"I never said it was, it's just that all of sudden, I have this urge to do it."

"Mom, I just don't want you to get on there and say a bunch of stuff that will make Kara feel worse than she already does. That's what I'm worried about."

"Of course. I'm very aware of that and extremely selective about what I say to people. I always have Kara in mind when talking to someone about it."

"Well, I guess I know what you mean. But just watch it."

"I will and I love you for trying to be so protective of your sister. Thanks, Tim."

"That's OK. Anyway, I am getting to be famous."

"What do you mean?"

"Now I have a father who is in jail and a mother who is going to be on TV telling everyone about it – so that sort of makes me famous, don't you think?"

Kate could only put her arm around him at that point and give him a big hug, which he tried to wiggle out of. He was still 17, and still embarrassed by a hug from Mom. She was so glad she had her boys – both of them were growing into compassionate and well mannered young men, and for that, she was extremely proud. On her previous trips to the jail, she realized that many of the women her age who were visiting inmates were there seeing their sons/ daughters. It was bad enough that her husband was there, but he was an adult and had made his own decision to be there based on his actions. If she had a child who was there, who's to say how she would have handled it? Kate was just glad she didn't have to find out and hopefully, she never would.

Kate held the letter in her hand, a little unsure of what it was going to say and proceeded to open it slowly, as if trying to ignore the inevitable.

Dear Ms. Nelson:

Thank you for replying so quickly to our invitation to appear on our daily noon-time show. As you know, the topic of the show will be MEN WHO ABUSE AND THE WOMEN WHO LOVE THEM — OR DID.

Kate was glad they added the last two words or she wouldn't have been able to appear on the show in good conscience. She sure didn't want anyone to think that she still loved Don, at least not like before. That part of her life was over and she was always happy to tell people how she truly felt about him. When she did let her feelings be known, she always seemed happier and ready to face this thing. It was her way of coping with a situation so completely draining, both mentally and physically. At least the visits to Don were becoming less and less frequent because going there was starting to make her uncomfortable, because she was forced to face how she felt about Don. At home, she could get away from it, turn on some soothing music, have a cup of tea and although the situation was never very far from her mind, each day she got a little better at accepting it. Their relationship had changed for the worse and she didn't have any regrets. On those rare occasions when she was having second thoughts, all she had to do was remember that her own daughter was the victim at the hands of her father and Kate had no trouble hating him all over again. With that thought in mind, it was easy.

She wondered who the other guests on the show would be and what they would admit in front of a TV camera. Kate felt like she had a lot of information to share, but at the same time, she didn't know if she wanted to air all her dirty laundry in public. With Don in jail now anyway, and most of the town knowing about it, wasn't most of the damage to the family's reputation already ruined? Even so, it wasn't her reputation she was worried about, it was her sanity. Yet, there were some issues she was eager to talk about, such as the ability to hold a family together when you have a husband who is in jail. It was the core of her very existence: how to keep the kids safe and happy during all of this upheaval.

Kate worried about Kara's reaction to her going on the show. She had a good relationship with her daughter, but Kara remained quiet through all of this, which was her own way of dealing with it. Kate never wanted to bring up the subject of the whole thing with her for fear of upsetting her, and at the same time, she worried about not talking to her about it, for fear of Kara thinking she didn't care about her feelings. Most of the time, Kate didn't say anything to her unless Kara brought it up to her first. The mother in her tried to keep things as normal as she could for her only daughter and hoped that would take her mind off everything else. Kate never knew what Kara was thinking, but she didn't really need to know because she deserved at least that much privacy and Kate wasn't going to hound her about it. Kate could take a lot, but it was doing her some good too, not having to think or talk about it all the time. She knew the best way to handle it was to let Kara do the talking, if and when she felt like it. Kate was there to guide and comfort her, not to pressure her into talking when she didn't want to. She knew Kara would open up when she was ready. That's the way Kate wanted it and so far, it was working out just fine.

CHAPTER NINE

Don wiggled around on the undersized bed trying to get comfortable and catch a few hours sleep. Calling it a bed was a stretch, it was more like a cot with a very thin mattress. He was sure that the constant back and neck pain he suffered was caused by the piece of junk that should have been thrown away years ago. It hadn't taken him long to realize that the more he slept, the better, because at least while he was sleeping, he didn't have to face the noise and the confusion of his grim surroundings. In his own mind, his sleeping more had another advantage; he thought it would make him more presentable to Kate, should she show up for a visit. He was never sure when she would show up, but when she did, they let him know she was there and they would escort him to where she was. He knew it wasn't easy for her to come there and for that, he felt sorry for her. She had the kids to worry about, her job, keeping the household going while he wasn't there and just the stress of having to do it all alone. He guessed she was somehow managing and Kate never complained. He wanted to know how she was doing, really doing, but they never seemed to either have the energy or the desire to discuss the things that were most important to either of them.

The lack of privacy and time also had something to do with it. The last thing he wanted was to look sleep-deprived in front of her. He wanted to look his best for her. But little did he know that Kate had already gotten to the point of no return as far as Don was concerned. Kate no longer cared what Don looked like or if he was able to get enough sleep before seeing her. It was going to take him longer than it took her to realize their relationship (if there was one) had entered a new phase. For her, it was all she could do just to tolerate him. After all that had happened, no one could blame her for feeling like she did. If something had to be done concerning the case, she did it out of duty, not her sincere desire to help. Don saw Kate's doing those things as proof that she still loved him so he was secure in knowing things hadn't changed that much between them. He was wrong.

Don's days had developed into an eerie sameness, there wasn't much change from one day to the next and he really had nothing to look forward to, except for Kate's visits. At least for now, it didn't seem likely he would get out of jail anytime soon and since getting there, he was settled with the fact he was probably here for the long haul. He didn't even waste his time asking any questions because there was no definite answer of when he could expect to be released. It was futile asking his attorney because he didn't know either. Don tried to concentrate on other things, like surviving. He was actually doing pretty well with that, but it was only because he stayed to himself and stayed out of the way. So many times he'd seen arguments and fights between inmates and they could get nasty and he always hoped no one would get seriously hurt before a guard would come running to break it up. It was a whole different world inside these gray walls — a world full of noise and anger, neither of which could ever be controlled.

Kate smoothed her black pencil skirt, looking at herself in the mirror again and giving herself the once over. Did she look good enough to be on TV? As the time got closer to appear on the show, she suffered a bad case of nerves and wondered if she was doing the right thing. She told herself it wasn't too late to back out and maybe that's exactly what she should do, all the while worrying people would see her on the show and start talking about her. She told herself they were talking about her now, so what was the difference? Quickly, she put that thought out of her mind and told herself she would be fine, but she didn't fully believe it.

"Lori?"

"KATE!!! How are you? I haven't heard from you lately and I was starting to worry. I am so glad you called!"

"I only have a few minutes to talk."

"Oh, you always say that".

"No, really. I am at the television station and we are about to tape the show that will be shown today at noon. Oh Lori, I am not sure of all of this. Why did I ever think doing it would be OK? Am I crazy?"

"No, you're not crazy, just a little tired. You have so much going on right now, that's all it is."

"Are you sure?"

"Of course I'm sure. You'll be fine."

"I have to go, they are calling for us."

"Kate don't worry and break a leg!"

"Isn't that only for when you're in a play?"

"I'm not sure, all I know is you'll knock 'em dead with what you have to say. Good luck, you'll be great."

"I wish I was as sure of that as you are."

"Bye, Kate. Just think before you answer the question and be yourself."

"Thanks, Lori. I always feel better when I talk to you. Bye."

Kate was lucky to have a sister like Lori. Always the strong one, always the rock for the both of them and always the one to be counted on in time of crisis, and if this wasn't a crisis, what was?

It was a crisis of many proportions, it affected each one of them differently and each had their own personal reaction to it. Kate thought being on the show would serve her well; it would hopefully put an end to the rumors and if people were going to talk about it, she would rather they had the right information. Kate knew that at this point in the case, people had already made up their minds as to what they thought and seeing a noonday news show probably wouldn't change their opinion. All Kate knew is that she was satisfied with what she was doing and she didn't have to answer to anyone. Don was the one who had put her in an awkward situation. She'd show him that she was strong enough to find her way out of it. The most important thing was that she didn't care if he approved the way she was going to do it or not. It really didn't matter to her what he thought because she had the right to do what she wanted, when she wanted.

The only one she had to answer to was herself and she was starting to really like it that way.

CHAPTER TEN

D on tried to get comfortable on the small plastic chair that was
in the room where he was allowed to watch TV for part of the
day. He was glad to get out of the cell for awhile but his back ached
from the bed he had and there was was no relief as he tried to balance
himself on the chair. With arms folded in front of him, he stared at the
TV screen. He just couldn't believe it! There was Kate – on TV – what
the heck was she doing? His eyes grew larger as he sat mesmerized and
felt as if he was glued to the chair. Did he actually see what he thought
he was seeing or was his mind playing tricks on him? No, as he focused
once again on the TV screen, he saw it was definitely Kate and he motioned the other guys to be quiet so he could get to hear Kate speak.

"Shut up you guys, that's my wife on the screen!"

The other inmates looked at him in disbelief.

"Get out! Hey, man your wife is hot!"

At that comment, Don jumped out of the chair and was about to
grab the other guy by the collar when a guard ran over to prevent any
trouble before it got started.

"What are you trying to do, Nelson?"

"He just saw my wife on the TV and said she was hot. I was going
to teach him a lesson."

"Sit down and you're not going to teach anybody anything."

Don sat down but vowed to get the guy the next time he saw him
and had the chance. He would remember him. Don turned once again
to the TV and became engrossed in listening to what Kate had to say.

The moderator began with, "Our next guest is Kate Nelson. Kate's
husband is currently in jail on a sexual battery charge and the alleged

victim is her daughter, or should I say their daughter, who is 12 years old. Kate, let me first welcome you to the show and we appreciate your taking the time to be with us today."

Kate answered with a weak, "Thank you."

"I'm sorry you have to go through this. Please tell the audience how you are dealing with it and how you are keeping your sanity through it all."

"Well, I don't know if I am, actually. I sometimes wonder."

Don was thinking, "Good answer. Keep the answers short and sweet. Don't give too much information. That way, no one will know more than they have to."

"Kate, I imagine that having your husband in jail has been a tremendous strain on your family – on many levels. What would you say has been the hardest thing to deal with in all of this?"

"Probably the effect all of this has had on my children. I guess I should say not only has it been hard to realize that their dad is in jail and why he is there, but having to take the ridicule of friends and neighbors when the kids had absolutely nothing to do with it. I can take a lot of the heat because of it, but I get angry when my children are punished for something that was totally out of their control. I have found out that both children and adults alike can be incredibly cruel, but you would think the adults would know better."

At this point, Don wanted to just hang his head and die. It was hard enough to face the fact that he was in jail for something he said he did not do, but even worse, was the fact that he was the reason his kids were suffering. Here he was locked up in this God forsaken place (although the jail chaplain would try to convince them otherwise) and all the while wondering how the kids were doing and he was probably about to find out, but did he have the strength to hear the truth?

The guys in the room with him all of a sudden looked at him with disgust. He couldn't tell exactly what they were thinking, but he could tell it wasn't good, whatever it was. He felt like a child who wanted to put his hands over his ears and not hear the truth. It was easy enough when you were a child to make that work for you, but now, all these years later, you had to figure out something else. So many times he could remember his mother saying, "These are the best years of your life" when she was referring to his youth. Everything was so simple back then, and those days were never coming back. He wondered if he would ever be able to untangle the mess he had gotten himself into and ever live a normal life again. It was a scary thought because he couldn't come up with a good answer to it. He hoped it would happen, but based on all the things going on around him, he doubted it ever would. He turned his head toward the blaring television and tried to catch the rest of what Kate was going to say.

"Can you elaborate on that, Mrs. Nelson?"

"The children are being treated unfairly in school not only by their peers, but by some of the school officials as well. Of course, some of them have been wonderful through all of this and we love them for it, but not enough of them. I am about at the point where I feel like going down there myself and letting them have a piece of my mind, what's left of it. I will go to any length to protect my kids from harm. All I do know is that once you start bothering my kids, be prepared for me to start bothering you, and I was raised on the streets of New York, so I'm pretty good at it. If I were you, I wouldn't want to come up against me."

"Hey Nelson, you got a pretty feisty little wife there, hah? She looks all nice and high society like, but I bet she's a tiger in bed. Is she, is she?"

"Why, you dirty little piece of crap. You take it back or I'll put my fist down your throat and we'll see how you like the taste of that!"

One of the prison guards in the room came running over and held Don's arm back so he couldn't land a punch.

"C'mon Nelson, you're coming wit' me."

"To where?"

"Back to your cell."

"But I'm not finished watching that TV show. My wife is one of the guests and that guy said something nasty about her."

"Sorry about that but rules is rules and you go back to your cell and cool off. I'm not about to have a fight break out in there. Not on my watch."

Don felt like putting his fist through the wall, he was so mad at himself for losing his temper because it made him miss the rest of the show with Kate. Not only was it a shock to find out that Kate had been on television in the first place, but to hear in her own words that the kids were suffering because of him was really hard to take. He couldn't even imagine what life must be like for them now and it was all because of him. What was wrong with him? He was the one who was supposed to love and protect them from stuff like this and here he was the one who had caused it. He was a poor excuse for a father and not only did Kate and the kids know it, but now the other inmates did too, which could only mean more trouble for him later. Absolutely nothing in his life was good, conditions like these are what made inmates kill themselves because there was nothing left to live for. It made for a sad and ugly world and he was stuck in the middle of it with no way to get out. He hung his head in despair all the time realizing he had really done it this time, and no high powered lawyer could get him released. He had to face the fact that he was here for awhile yet and no amount of begging to his lawyer or to Kate could change that. He was here to stay and the best thing to do now was keep his ears and eyes open and his mouth shut.

He turned over on the bed trying to forget the nightmare that had begun only a few short months ago and realized he hadn't dreamt it; he was living it.

CHAPTER ELEVEN

Ken Higgins met unexpectedly with Don and that made him a little uneasy.

"Mr. Nelson, how are you?"

"As you can figure, I've been better."

"I'm sure, but I came down to see you this morning because I wanted to give you an update on the case. I'd much rather discuss it in person than in a letter. As you know, since the judge denied bail, you have to stay here for awhile. But in the meantime, we are working hard on your case. By that I mean we are getting witness lists together, preparing to set up depositions to help build our case and eventually doing the things leading up to the trial. What I do expect is to get a plea offer from the State Attorney's office any time now. Based on that, we can discuss the terms of the plea offer and if we think it is in your best interest to accept it or go to trial."

"Would accepting a plea offer mean I would get a long jail term?"

"I don't know. I won't know that for sure until I receive the offer. All I can tell you know is I expect it any day now and I will let you know something as soon as I get the information. I had to see some other clients here and thought I would come by so you would know what was happening and that we haven't just been sitting on your case. I'm sure that's what you've been thinking, but unfortunately, the system moves very slowly and we are at the mercy of the court as to how fast we get answers."

"Call me stupid, but what does it mean when we get a plea offer? I think what I know what it is, in general, but what I want to know is what it will mean to my case if I get one."

Ken continued with, "A plea offer is just that — it means they will suggest terms of the plea, such as so many years in jail, probation, etc. in lieu of having a trial. If we accept a plea, it means there will be no trial."

"Oh, I see. I wasn't aware that's what it meant. That sounds great, not having to go to trial."

"Right, but what you have to remember is that it can backfire on you, too. Say you accept a plea and decide not to go to trial. You are taking a chance that the offer would be better than what you would end with by having a trial. Don't forget that sometimes we have to throw in a sympathy vote. If we a lucky enough to get a jury made up of old ladies who have a son your age with a family, that's the kind of juror who would likely rule in your favor. On the other hand, if we get a bunch of men with pre-teen daughters, the sympathy from them just isn't going to be there. So it turns out to be one of those things you have to weigh very carefully before deciding what to do."

"Great. Now I am more confused than ever."

"Of course, I also want you to understand that just because we get an offer, that doesn't always mean it will be in your best interest. I won't know that till I can read it for myself and see what it says. I'm hoping for an offer that might be good for you because it will spare you and the family from being at a trial. Not only that but since this is your first offense, we may have a good shot. It's all up to the State Attorney and unfortunately, we are at his mercy."

Don couldn't say he was surprised after hearing what his attorney had to say. Lately none of the news he ever got was good so this was just more information to go alone with all the other bad news. He told himself maybe there was an outside chance that he might actually get a good plea offer. He also knew the problem was that his charge was so offensive to most people that even a first charge of this nature didn't speak well for him. Who ever heard someone with a charge of sexual battery on a child under 12 getting a good deal? It was naïve to even think that would happen. Don might as well face it, he was cooked, pure and simple. No doubt about it, he was screwed — and not in a good way.

With each passing day, Don began to sink deeper into the throes of despair. There was no motivation to be hopeful, everything he heard about him or his case was negative. Lately, he seriously questioned Kate's loyalty, too. He wanted to believe only the best about her, but her actions proved otherwise. First on his mind was the fact that her visits were getting more and more infrequent. That told him she was losing interest in the visits and more likely, interest in him. He had nothing but time on his hands, so he wondered if he was just imagining it. With everything else he'd lost, he didn't want to lose Kate and the kids, too. He understood that bringing them to the jail with her was not in their best interest and he agreed with Kate's decision to not have them come there to visit. His heart told him just the opposite; that he did long to see the kids but in order to keep the peace, he kept quiet and didn't let Kate know his true feelings about it. To do so would have only made things worse between them, and he definitely didn't want that. He knew that if there was any chance at all of having Kate continue to love him as her husband, he had to be on his best behavior and keep his thoughts to himself as to what he felt about seeing the kids. He was still hopping mad about Kate's decision to go on that talk show, but he knew he had to downplay his reaction and keep his comments in check. The best thing he could hope for now was to have her keep visiting him at the jail, no matter the frequency, because once that stopped, he would be hard pressed to keep himself in her good graces. That's when he would really be in bad shape, and if that did happen, he wasn't sure if he would have the energy and the fight within him to make things right again. That would remain to be seen.

In the days ahead, he decided his best course of action was to not to make any waves and listen to everyone who told him what to do: the jail, Kate and his attorney. All of sudden he felt like he was the bad child and this was his punishment and now to atone, he had to listen to everyone, with no screw-ups. That's the thing that would get him in trouble and he had enough of that already. His best plan of action was no action, let everyone else act for him, and they would because they'd been doing it since he was in here. He had no say in anything of consequence, nothing he thought of on his own came to fruition anyway, so he let everyone else take over, it was easier that way.

He was too frustrated and too down to put up much of a fight so when things got too hard to handle, he would lie down on the bed, roll over and go to sleep because it took the pain away for hours at a time. Sleeping was his coping mechanism, his comfort and his escape, and for now, it was all he had.

CHAPTER TWELVE

Kate woke up to a morning full of sunshine and possibilities, a morning where she felt so good that she almost forgot the turmoil she was in. She knew that a lot had to happen before it would all be over, but this morning, for some reason, she felt well and rested and was looking forward to the day.

She sat on the back deck of her sprawling Florida home stretching her legs and allowing the sun to penetrate and warm her skin. Her steaming cup of coffee was the perfect accompaniment to her croissant, which she picked up early this morning after she dropped the kids off at school. Her work schedule had eased somewhat and she was now able to work only 2 or 3 days a week. Luckily, she had sold a few houses in the last months, so she was using the commissions on those sales to live on and pay the bills. She knew that the savings account was available to her, but she wanted to see if she could manage on her own.

Taking care of herself and the kids gave her a great sense of pride and independence, because she didn't want to rely on the savings account. The way things might turn out, if Don had to stay in jail for any length of measurable time, she knew she would have to come up with a plan on how they would survive without his income and so far, she was dealing with it. Having to work less gave her more time to spend with the kids and more time to devote to all the matters of Don's case. It would have been the start of a perfect day if it had been only a few months ago, before everything changed, before she realized from the moment Don was arrested, life as her family knew it, would never be the same.

On a beautiful day like this, Kate dismissed any further thought of jail, Don and anything to do with the two of those. This was to be a day to enjoy without any negative thoughts to ruin it. Kate decided nothing was going to stop her from relishing in the weather and her positive outlook, at least for one whole day. She deserved the break from everything else that was going on around her.

Kate felt like having lunch with her friend, Sue, because they hadn't connected in so long with all the latest commotion at the Nelson house. She dialed Sue's number and was relieved when she answered the phone.

"Hello?"

"Sue, it's Kate. I have a free day today and thought you might want to meet me for lunch."

"That would be great. I just need to be home by the time Becky gets off the school bus so I can drive her to her violin lesson".

"That's no problem. I have to be home early enough to pick up Kara. I have been doing that lately instead of having her take the bus home. It has been better for the both of us. This way, I don't have to worry about the kids on the bus giving her a hard time on the way home. With the boys staying after school most days, it's just Kara and I in the afternoons. I think it's brought us closer and sometimes, we even stop for an ice cream on the way home and she loves that. She deserves at least that much."

"I know. The poor little thing. You will just have to keep a close eye on her and make sure she is OK. You'll know when she's not being herself."

"Yeah, that's why I think picking her up from school has really helped. It gives us a chance to talk when we are completely alone."

"That's good."

"OK, well, do you have any preference on which restaurant you want to go to?"

"No, not really, I'm open to anywhere really, I'm just glad to get out of the house for some adult conversation for a change."

"How about we meet at 12:30 at O'Hara's Pub? Would that be alright with you?"

"Sure, I'll see you then."

Kate decided to wear a pair of khaki colored pants and a dusty rose colored blouse with a scoop collar. It was casual yet classy, which was just the look she was going for. That was her exact sense of style, casual-chic, but always knew how to add some piece to give the overall outfit a certain flair. She wasn't a jeans type of woman except when at a sporting event or out in the garden cleaning up the yard. Wherever she went or whatever she wore, she always tried to look her best. She took pride in her appearance and tried to instill that in the kids, too. She was the type of woman who looked good in anything because it had a lot to do with her attitude as well. Up till recently, she was happy with her life and she didn't have many worries. That fact would show through to those around her. Now that was reversed and her life was the problem because things were so up in the air about Don and what was eventually going to happen with him. Until they knew that for sure, nothing could be counted on. The dragging on of his case had put her and the kids in limbo. They had turned into puppets of the system and only the legal system held the strings. When the system said dance, you did. You had no other choice if you wanted the case to keep moving along and not be stalled.

While Don was in jail, at least she had the luxury of not having to worry about what would happen when he got out. She was telling the kids he would be out at some point, she just didn't know when right now, that part was true. The part that wasn't true was saying he would eventually be out of jail. She had no idea on earth if that statement contained any semblance of truth, but for now, she was sticking to it for the kids' sake. She didn't think this was the time to open a can of worms with them and tell them she had a feeling that the case wasn't going all that well. The twins seemed to hold their judgment in reserve because it seemed they had mixed feelings. They loved their father and wanted him back home, but when they realized why he was out of the house all this time, their anger flared. They hated their father at the same time they loved him, which would be hard for any child to deal with, no matter what their age. They hated him for making everything so hard on their mother and they vowed to Kate that they would do anything they could to protect Kara from him.

Kate wondered if judges sometimes made provisions to keep a person in jail because the victim lived in the same home. That was something she was going to talk to Ken Higgins about. He would know the answer, Kate just wasn't sure if she wanted to hear it. If she was a weak person or she had let herself, this whole thing could have been a living nightmare. Not that it was all that far from it now, but at least the four of them were safe and sound, with no wolves at the door. If she could manage to say that at the end of this mess, she would have done her job, and done it well. Then she would be able to hold her head up high and face those who mocked her and her children. To those who showed their support and stayed by their side, she would publicly thank them. To those who were so quick to jump the gun and spout off their mouth when they had no idea what they were talking about, let them be damned.

She waved to Sue when she saw her enter the restaurant and motioned for her to come to the table. The two women embraced lightly and took their seats.

"Oh, Kate, it's so good to see you!"

"Thanks. I'm so glad you were able to make it today on such short notice."

"Well, once I put Becky on the school bus in the morning, I can figure out what I want to do from there."

"Must be nice; my life used to be like that! These days, I wonder if my life will ever be normal again. Some days when I think about it, I'm not so sure.

Every now and then I have a day when I want to put the pillow over my head, pull up the covers and not move. I guess I shouldn't complain, because a lot of people have it a lot worse than I do."

"Kate, no matter what you have going on in your life you have your bad and good days. I know."

"This whole thing is just starting to grate on me".

"I don't doubt it."

"Hey, Sue, let's order and not worry about the other stuff."

"Sounds good".

With that, their waiter appeared and he asked for their order. They gave him their selections and proceeded to start a conversation, which was the basis of the lunch in the first place.

"So Kate, tell me how you're doing. I mean really tell me."

"I'm OK, really."

"Look, I've known you for a long time; you don't have to hide anything from me. You might do that with other people but not me."

"I know. It's just that I am constantly bombarded with it. No matter what is going on at the moment, or even if nothing is going on, it's always there. I don't know how to sweep it under the rug and have it stay there. I guess I can't."

"Sure you can. Why don't you come over to my place when you feel like that? A change of scenery would probably do you good."

"Probably, but the last thing I want to do is bother you when you are trying to work at home now."

"Don't worry about me. I'll be fine. Believe me, I am caught up right now, so I have the time to spare. Some days I just find myself watching the clock till Becky comes home so there'll be another thing to focus my attention on."

"Are you kidding? I used to have days like that, but no more. Sometimes I wonder if I'll ever have days like that again."

"Of course you will. It's just going to take a little time. You have to be patient. You know how the justice system works – slow!"

"Tell me about it. It's as if I'm in that tortoise and the hare cartoon and I'm the tortoise. Only in my version, I still finish last."

They both laughed as they were finishing up their meal. Kate always felt good around Sue because she could be herself. There was no pretense and no expectations. Sometimes just being around a person she felt comfortable with helped Kate cope. It was nice to let someone else be in control for a little while, even though she was more than capable. That was her, good ole capable Kate, but it was getting old and she secretly cursed every time she was feeling frustrated. This was all his fault. He was the one who had put them in this position, but Kate knew she was the one who was going to get them out of it, whether Don was with them or not.

When Kate got home that afternoon, she felt good physically. Having a light healthy lunch seemed to sit well with her and she was especially conscious of keeping herself well. There was too much going on to let anything interfere with her health. What would happen to the kids if something happened to her? She didn't want to think about it because right now, she was all they had. That was reason enough to keep going.

CHAPTER THIRTEEN

State of Florida vs. Donald Nelson
Case No.: 2009 CF 22346784B
<u>PLEA OFFER</u>
30 Months incarceration in county jail
$1,200.00 court costs
5 years probation
Register as sexual predator

"I think you should take it."

"Why? That's a lot of jail time. The other stuff I can deal with, well, maybe except the last one. I think it's too long. I'm not all that agreeable to it."

"I understand. You have to look at it from another angle, too. As your attorney, it is my job to advise you in things like this and I think this offer is the better of what you will end up with if you take it to trial."

"I thought I'd have a better chance taking it to trial because I could explain my side."

"I know. But let me tell you something first: it is always dangerous for the defendant to take the stand, no matter what's at stake. So, let's get that out of the way by saying I'm against it."

"Listen, when you are facing a charge such as this one, there's not going to be a lot of sympathetic ears in the courtroom. What you do want is to get yourself the best deal you can. I would advise that you accept this plea, not only because it will avoid having to take this case to trial, but will be better for Kate and the kids, too. Plus, even if you did go to trial, you can never predict how twelve other people will view the case. You could very likely get a much worse deal and although I know you don't like the idea of the jail time, you will receive credit for time already served and this is probably the lesser of two evils, considering you may be facing much more time after the trial."

"Now I'm more unsure than ever what to do. But the thing I don't like about the whole thing is that no matter what I decide to do, people will think I am guilty."

"I always tell my clients to take a good long hard look at themselves and what they did or didn't do to get themselves in here. If you can tell yourself with a straight face that you are 100% innocent, then by all means make it known to the public. If not, take the least amount of time offered, do that time, and get on with your life. It is the best advice I have for you at this point."

"I guess you're right. OK, I'll take the plea."

"I will go back to my office and have the proper paperwork prepared. Once that is finished, I will come back down here and have you sign it. After that, we will file it with the court and it will be official. Then we will present it at the plea hearing, which is about a month from now, I will check on the exact date and let you know."

"Alright. I guess that's as good as I can hope for. I am not too thrilled with it, but if I don't take it, I could end up with something worse, and I don't need that."

"I'll be back in a few days with the document for you to sign and we will go from there."

With that, Don and his attorney shook hands and Ken headed toward the exit.

Don understood what was happening but that didn't make it any easier to swallow. He knew now that he was at a point of no return. There would be nobody to listen to him at a trial, nobody to listen to his attorney argue the fact that he was innocent, nobody to listen and realize he had no prior criminal record and nobody to listen for the most important reason of all, that nobody wanted to listen because nobody cared.

Kate showed she didn't really care because the frequency of her visits had dwindled down to almost none and the times she did come and see him seemed to be because she needed his input about the household duties or bills. It was never about him, and his needs. It was always about something else that he had nothing to do with, and he didn't feel was important, as long as he was locked away from everything and everyone he knew.

The kids showed they didn't really care because they never came to see him anymore and they never even wrote letters asking if he was doing OK. Nothing; it was as if any contact he did have with them was suddenly cut off and remained that way.

His job showed they didn't really care because they decided that after a review of his situation, they would have no choice but to fire him. Who could blame them? What company would want to hold onto an employee that was unable to physically be in the office, no matter what the reason? Not only that, but they didn't want the publicity of anyone knowing they kept him on the payroll despite the fact that he was in jail on a sexual battery charge. It would be a black mark on the company and they didn't want that, either. So the decision was made that the best choice of action was to let him go. If Don had made a mess of things for himself, that was his business. They wanted no reflection of what he did on them.

His group of baseball parents showed they didn't really care by telling him they were resigning him in his current position because he "no longer presented a positive image and good role model" to the kids who looked up to him, or used to. Don understood their thinking, but he was disappointed nonetheless. Obviously, he know that at the moment he couldn't be part of the group, but just the fact that he would no longer be associated with them was depressing to him. He had been so much a part of the group for so long that now it was going to be a big adjustment to come to terms with the fact he no longer had anything to do with them. He thought it would never come to this.

Piece by piece, his life was crumbling around him and all he could do was watch it happen. It was as if this dark, cold and uncaring world was sucking him into it and he no longer had the strength to fight back. He wanted to give up and as he crawled onto the thin mattress feeling the springs jam into his back, he knew for the next few years his life as he'd known it was over. No more Kate, kids, job, community leader, etc., he was now reduced to being just a number in the judicial system, an inmate, one with no rights and no privacy. Everything had been stripped from him and he'd have to wait years to get them back. The decision, though not yet final, had been made and he was going to be here for a long time, and there was nothing anyone could do to change it.

His best course of action was to just resign himself to the fact and not play the "if only" game. If only I didn't get caught when I did, if only I didn't alienate Kate and the kids through all of this, if only I didn't have to suffer the guilt of it all and the biggest "if only" of all, if only I was innocent.

CHAPTER FOURTEEN

Kara walked listlessly around the house and Kate asked her if anything was wrong. And she answered with a dull "No.....not really." That was Kara's understated way of saying that yes, something was wrong, and Kate wouldn't know unless she took the steps to pull it out of her.

Kate started with, "Kara, you know you can tell me anything. I mean anything. You never have to be afraid to tell me what's bothering you and I will always try to help you. If I can't help you, I promise I will find someone who will. You understand that, don't you?"

"Uh-huh."

"OK. I think there is something you want to say but you're a little unsure how to start to tell me. Am I right?"

"Yeah, kind of."

"Well, how about if I mention some stuff and then you tell me if you want to talk about it further. Would that be an easier way for you to get it out?"

"I don't know."

"OK, well, let's try it. Is it something here at home?"

"No."

"Is it something about your friends?"

"Not my good friends."

At this point, Kate was a little unsure of where to go with this. It had something to do with the kids her own age. Kate could figure out that much so she continued to tiptoe around Kara, hoping she would hit on it soon.

"Is it something about the other kids at school, the ones who aren't your friends?"

"Yeah, but it's kind of hard to explain."

"OK, but I think we're getting somewhere. Are some of the kids at your school bothering you about what is happening with Dad?"

"Sometimes they do. Most of them are nice about it or don't say anything at all. But there's a small group of kids who can be really mean. They say nasty stuff to me sometimes as I'm walking down the hall."

"Can you me an example of what kind of stuff so I know what you are talking about?"

"Well, it's kind of mean, so I don't know if you want me to tell you or not."

That's Kara, always worried about everyone else's feelings and not her own. Here she is as the victim in this case and she's worried about her mother! Kate wanted to take Kara in her arms and give her a big bear hug. But she knew Kara wouldn't like it right now, so the best thing was to keep the conversation going because with Kara, those conversations could be few and far between.

Kate continued with, "Of course I want you to tell me. You know I am always saying that you can tell me anything.

"Go ahead, say what you were going to tell me."

"OK…"

Kara hesitated and Kate could tell it was going to be hard for her. So to ease the pressure on her, Kate invited Kara to sit next to her on the couch and told Kara to continue.

"Well, remember that history test I had?"

Kate said, "Yes, I remember how hard you studied for it and that you were worried about it. I know that I tried to quiz you on some of the stuff that might be on the test."

"When we got the test papers back, I was happy I got a B. But then when I walking down the hallway to go to the cafeteria for lunch, some boy that I didn't know came up to me and said some mean things."

"What mean things?"

"He said, "Hey, Kara, I bet you thought the test was hard, or did you think it was easy? Ya' know, Easy --- just like you.""

"Are you kidding me? I'll take care of that. I'll find out who it is and make sure that from now on he keeps his mouth shut."

"But how are you going to find out?"

"Don't worry about that, I will."

"Then what are you going to do?"

"I'm not sure yet, you just leave that to me. I don't want you to worry about anything. I will take care of it."

That's what Kara was afraid of. She knew Kate; she knew what Kate was capable of when others tried to ruffle her feathers. But when the others were bothering her children, that was a whole different ball game and that's one game Kate didn't intend to lose. Kate couldn't even believe the audacity of this kid, whoever he was. She was making it her business to find out, and she would, whether the kid liked it or not. She hoped his parents were ready for it, too, because they were going to get an earful as well and Kate couldn't wait. Sometimes, when you wanted justice, you had to go out and get it yourself and that was Kate's most immediate plan.

Kate was fired up inside because of what Kara had just told her. She was so upset that she decided to take a walk to the mailbox to cool off. Maybe that would settle her down, but maybe not in light of how crazy this whole thing had made her. She was starting to get a headache and it had a tight grip on her mental being, as well as her physical one. Damn you Don, this is your fault. You were the one who put the kids in this position and the one who made their everyday life so difficult.

Congratulations, you're a real Father of the Year.

CHAPTER FIFTEEN

Kate stretched out on the couch in the living room flipping through the day's assortment of mail. There was the usual number of bills, advertisements for things they didn't want or need, a sale flyer from the local grocery store and one very interesting letter that Kate focused on. It was a letter from Kara's school. Kate fumbled with the flap of the envelope, trying to quickly rip it open. She unfolded the white piece of paper and started to read it.

Dear Mr. and Mrs. Nelson:

Those very words struck Kate as odd, because lately, if she was addressed as Mrs. Nelson it was to her alone, not Don. Most everyone knew he was in jail by now anyway, so this was very strange to her. Then she thought it was just a formality on the part of the school, that no matter where Don was, the school was covering itself so as to include both parents on anything that had to do with Kara. Kate realized later it wasn't the school's responsibility to keep track of where Don was. They had plenty to do without worrying about where to send a letter; the address that was on file at the school is the one they would use.

Because Kate's life was so complicated right now, she just assumed everyone else was consumed with what was going on, too. That wasn't exactly what was happening. Her friends and family had their own lives to lead and their own problems to deal with. Why would Kate think that just because her circumstances were a little more serious than theirs that they should be just as concerned with what was going on with her? With a question like that, Kate hoped she wasn't "losing it". She had prided herself in taking on all the responsibility of the house, the kids, the vehicles and the criminal case; which was only getting worse. She just needed to realize that her problems were hers alone and she was the only one who should be dealing with them. Sure, everyone told her that they felt sorry for her, but that didn't mean they would be at her front doorstep ready to knock it down with offers to help. She knew better than that and she also knew that having people tell you they would help and having them actually do it was two different things.

Kate sat down on the couch with the envelope from the school in hand as she prepared herself for what it might say.

"Here goes nothing", she thought to herself. As she ripped along the back flap of the envelope she tried to brace herself for what she was going to read. It read:

Dear Mrs. Nelson:

We are aware of the fact that your husband is in jail and we understand that this must be a terrible time for you and your children. Kara is a sweet child and we hope only the best for her.

As you know, our school psychologist has met with Kara and the psychologist seems to feel like Kara would benefit from counseling. However, that is not the reason for this letter.

Recently an incident occurred here at the school that was brought to our attention by a student and we feel you should be aware of it. We would like to discuss it with you in person to see if we can put our heads together to find an appropriate solution for all of us. We don't want to make this any more difficult on you than it already is, but at the same time, we want to make sure we are doing the best for Kara, as one of our best and brightest students.

Please contact our office at your earliest convenience so we can meet and discuss this matter further.

Thank you.

Sincerely,

Michael C. Barton, Principal

Kate put the letter in the pile of mail that was on her desk and didn't want to have to deal with it at the moment. There was so much going on that it was hard to concentrate on any one thing. She knew it needed attention but to delay it for just a little while wasn't going to hurt anyone, was it? The school might think so but she would do it in her own time, maybe tomorrow. She was in one of those moods where she felt if she read or heard one more thing about the case, she was going to scream. She was managing fairly well on her own, but every now and then, the stress of it all was overwhelming and she needed some time to herself. It didn't have to be hours at a time, she only needed but a few minutes. Those were the minutes she treasured, the minutes with a hot cup of tea in hand and as she sipped the hot tea from her favorite mug, the troubles of the world seemed to disappear. The only problem was that after drinking the tea, the problems were back again, bigger and brighter than ever.

The following day Kate found herself ready to tackle the pile of mail on her desk. She looked better and felt better than she did yesterday, so maybe that would give her the strength to deal with the paperwork. Kate picked up the school envelope and pulled out the letter. She was curious as to why they would want to talk to her. Had Kara done something that the school felt she should know about? Kara was not the type of kid to normally get in trouble, but who knows? Even good kids lost their way once in awhile. Kate hoped that wasn't the case now. Kate braced herself for what might come next as she picked up the phone.

"Good morning, Rosemont Middle School."

"Good morning. Can you connect me with the principal's office, please?"

"One moment."

A young girl answered with, "Mr. Barton's office."

"Yes, this is Kate Nelson and I received a letter from Mr. Barton asking me to make an appointment to come in and discuss a matter involving my daughter, Kara Nelson. She's in seventh grade, but I am not really sure what he wants to talk about."

"I'd be glad to make that appointment for you. Let's see............ can you come in tomorrow at 10:00?"

"Yes, that will be fine. I'll be there. Thank you."

"Just please let us know if you can't make it."

"I sure will and thank you."

OK, one potential disaster dealt with. Mark that one for Kate's side. Actually, the worst was yet to come because calling on the phone to make an appointment was just a little bit different than actually showing up at the appointment. That was going to really be fun! Kate wasn't a drinker, but if she was, she would have mixed herself a good stiff cocktail, one that burns the sides of your mouth and throat as it goes down. The kind that makes you grit your teeth and waits for you to take a breath of fresh air before doing it all over again to drown whatever sorrow you were trying to forget. This was a sorrow she couldn't forget; one that would be with her till her dying day. One that she swore she would get revenge for; even if that revenge had to be directed toward her own husband.

When he made the decision to hurt their child, that was all the ammunition Kate needed. His time would come and when it did, she hoped the world would be there to watch it. That would be the time when her head would truly be held high; when the world would know the real story, and because of it, the real pain she had to endure that few people knew about.

CHAPTER SIXTEEN

Kate walked tentatively up the courthouse steps and took a deep breath. If what she was feeling now was any indication of how she would feel at a trial, then she was glad there may not be one. With Don's decision to accept the plea offer, she and the kids would be spared the embarrassment and indignity of it all. The kids didn't need any more fuel to add to the already too big fire that goes with the stigma of having a parent in jail. Kate always kept them aware of what was happening with Don's case and as much as she wanted to shield them from it, they had a right to know. In fact, she had told them they were welcome to come to the plea hearing and as she expected, the twins refused and Kara had no desire to see Don right now, and Kate didn't blame her.

Kate tried to act nonchalant while at the courthouse, like she was there all the time. As she stepped into the elevator, she wondered if those around her recognized who she was and why she was there. Oh well, no matter, she was here now and she had to go through with it.

When the elevator stopped at the third floor and Kate made her way to the courtroom, she noticed Ken Higgins outside holding his briefcase.

"Hi Kate, good to see you."

"Thanks, you too. I'm not sure if I'm feeling a little strange being here, but I guess I'm OK. I have to be. Don't want to act like the sniveling little wife, you know, because that's really not me."

"I know, but you'll do just fine. You always do."

"What exactly is going to happen in there?"

"It's simple, really. Don will accept the plea when asked and then sign paperwork agreeing to the fact and that should wrap it up."

"That's all there is to it?"

"Yes, because he has already told me that is what he wants to do. Don knows a trial wouldn't be good for any of you, especially him. He understands that he has the right to a speedy trial, but that the verdict could be a lot worse than the plea offer. It's hard to find a jury that will be sympathetic to someone accused of sexual battery on their own daughter."

"I've tried to advise him the best I could and he's doing the right thing."

"I know, I just wish it were over."

"Don't worry. Once the hearing starts, it'll go fast."

Kate nodded her head and clutched her purse tightly and she kept saying to herself, "Please let this thing start so I can just go home and forget this whole thing ever happened."

The heavy mahogany door to the courtroom opened and the bailiff instructed that everyone come in and sit down. Ken led Kate to the front of the room and guided her to the first row. She thanked him as she sat down.

A few more people came in and she wondered who they were and why they would even want to come to something like this. She turned around nervously and didn't see anyone she knew, which was a small relief. When news of Don's case first broke, everyone was curious and was either talking to her or about her. Now that a few months had passed and it was "old news" maybe the public's interest in it had waned as well. In the beginning, it wasn't unusual for her to do simple errands and see people pointing at her and whispering behind her back. She would just go about her business, but still felt eerie about it just the same.

The door to the right of where the judge sat opened and in came the bailiff, leading Don to his place to sit. Kate thought she was going to need some fresh air. He was wearing the blue prison jumpsuit and the hardest thing for Kate to see was that he was chained at the wrists, waist and ankles. He looked straight at her and nodded and she had no other reaction but to stare back at him. He looked relatively well groomed, so that was a relief. Kate would have been upset if he looked like he needed a shower because that wasn't the way she knew him, after all these years. He was the type of man who even while in jail would want to keep himself presentable. It was just the way he was. Kate was glad to see that being in jail hadn't changed that part of him.

He was escorted to his seat and with the chains on him, he couldn't even reach up to his forehead and wipe away a stray hair. That was the part that unnerved her. She tried not to look at him and decided to focus her attention elsewhere. Kate couldn't ask the attorney anything because he was already in front of the courtroom sitting at the table near the judge.

The judge began with, "This is the case of the State of Florida vs. Donald Nelson. The judge then looked over at Don and said, "Mr. Nelson, I understand that you wish to enter a plea and that your attorney has explained what your signing that plea would mean. Is that correct?"

"Yes, your Honor, it is".

"I see. You do understand that by signing the plea offer you are giving up your right to a speedy trial and that you will serve out the terms of the plea offer in place of the trial, its verdict and corresponding punishment?"

"Yes, your Honor."

"Very well. Attorney Higgins, please bring the document over to the defendant for his signature."

Yes, your Honor."

Once Don signed the paper, Ken brought it back to the judge, he told those in the room that the plea hearing was concluded and that Mr. Nelson was now formally to serve the terms of the plea offer as follows:

30 months incarceration in county jail
$1,200.00 court costs
5 years probation
Register as sexual predator

The last one on the list was the one Kate was having a hard time with. Was she actually married to a sexual predator? It all sounded so ugly. Kate wouldn't wish the long lasting stigma of that on anyone, maybe not even Don. His first priority to deal with was his attitude about doing the time on the sentence. His having to register as a sexual predator would have to be dealt with later.

Kate watched the bailiff escort Don through the side door of the courtroom and stood up as Ken Higgins approached her.

"Kate, are you OK?"

"Oh yes, I'm fine. It's just a little overwhelming watching your husband tell a judge he is accepting a plea offer. All of this may hit me later. Right now I think I am just kind of numb."

"I hope you'll feel better later."

"I think I will, thanks."

"With that, Kate stepped into the elevator and Ken walked down the opposite hallway. Even though they were on opposite sides of Don's case, she could tell that Ken was genuinely nice man. Then she remembered that's how she used to describe her husband, too.

CHAPTER SEVENTEEN

Kate steered her car into the school parking lot, careful to watch out for kids who might not be looking where they were going. She was always very mindful of that fact whenever she found herself in a place where kids gather. The spot she found to park in was partially shaded, so at least her car wouldn't be burning hot inside when she came back. That was a trick she learned a long time ago when she first learned to drive. Living most of her life in Florida had made her aware of such things. Down here, the name of the game wasn't trying to park closest to where you needed to go; it was parking in the shade, no matter how far you had to walk to get there.

Kate got out of the car and walked into Kara's school. She headed for the main office as a young woman got up to greet her.

"Yes, can I help you?"

"I'm Mrs. Nelson and I have a 10:00 appointment to see Mr. Barton."

"OK. I will let him know you're here and please have a seat. Can I get you a cup of coffee?"

"No thanks, I'm fine."

Kate sat there and all of a sudden, she felt a little weak. Was it nerves? Was it because she didn't know what the meeting was about? Was it because she had to deal with the principal on her own? In situations like this, she usually had Don by her side to lean on, just in case. But Kate couldn't think about that now. He wasn't here, she was alone and she had to make the best of it. The kids were counting on her to do it, and deep down, she knew she could hold her own against anybody.

She watched as various students came into the office to ask the staff to help them saying they forgot their lunch money, had to call their mom because she needed her to come down and sign a permission slip, etc. Kate remembered those days when the kids were younger and she used to get calls like that. It was kind of cute watching the kids come in with their different stories.

"Mrs. Nelson, Mr. Barton will see you now."

"Thank you."

"Right this way."

Mr. Barton stood up from his desk and welcomed Kate to his office. She sat down and listened as he began to speak.

"Thank you for coming in to see me this morning. I appreciate your being so prompt in response to our letter. Please let me introduce you to Ms. Pratt, who is the school guidance counselor. I will let her explain to you why we asked you here."

"Mrs. Nelson, we are aware of the fact that your husband is in jail and we are sorry for what your family has to go through because of it. We also know that your daughter, Kara, is the victim in the case and this has to be a terrible time for you. It has recently been brought to our attention that because of this situation, it has caused some tension among Kara's peers."

"What do you mean, tension?"

"I did hear some nasty comments about your daughter and the case in general as I was walking down the hallway a few days ago. It was very upsetting. I was able to identify the student making those remarks and dealt with the situation. However, it has come to the point where this whole thing has been just too disruptive to the school in general."

"What do you mean? This isn't Kara's fault, you know. As you yourself just said, she is the victim here! What do you want her to do? Hide her head in the sand until this is all over? It could take years for this whole thing to be done with, but you are not going to make Kara feel as if any of this was her fault!"

Kate couldn't believe the nerve of the woman! She was nothing but a self-righteous bitch and Kate wasn't going to let her intimidate her. Just try it lady, and then you'll see who you're dealing with!

"I know how you feel."

"Oh you do? Have you ever had a daughter in this situation? Where every time you turn around you have to watch over your shoulder to see who is talking and gossiping about you? How do you think you would deal with all of that if you were the victim at twelve years old? Why don't you tell me, since you profess to know so much about it."

"Now Mrs. Nelson, I didn't mean to upset you, I am just trying to get the facts straight. What we have here is a situation that has never come up before so please be a little understanding and realize that this is all new to us, too. We are trying to keep a handle on it, but it is a difficult situation at best."

Yeah, lady? You don't know the half of it!

"Ms. Pratt, I believe the situation is difficult for all of us. However, maybe if the school made more of an effort to educate the students, not about the case itself, but maybe inform them of how hard this is on Kara they could deal with it better, too. Maybe you could explain to them that they can help her by not yelling nasty words and comments at her, but by including her in their activities so she feels she is a part of what is going on, things like that. I personally think that might be the way to go."

"Well, Mrs. Nelson, we've had some meetings on the subject and we feel this situation is getting a little out of hand and a little too big for us to handle."

"A little out of hand? It is only out of hand because you let it get that way. What kind of school is this anyway? Do you let the students dictate what you do? Do you let the students just run wild and say whatever they wish with no recourse?"

"Of course not. We just feel when we have a situation such as this, that maybe other means should be taken to settle it."

"Oh yeah, like what?"

Kate was getting a little hot under the collar and was on the verge of losing it. She didn't want to do that, but at the same time, she wasn't going to let this woman get to her or her daughter. Kate had a few more words for her if she kept on pressing the issue, making her feel like all of this was Kara's fault! Kate decided to continue to listen to her, but if she said one more thing that was out of line, Kate was going to let her have it.

"Actually, after the meetings and review of the entire situation, we did come up with a suggestion."

Kate was getting agitated by now and could hardly wait to hear what this woman would come up with next.

"Oh yeah, and what's that?"

"Maybe you would consider removing Kara from the school and placing her elsewhere. Perhaps even a private school where the students weren't as aware of the case as they are here."

"First off, I am NOT going to consider placing Kara elsewhere! This is her school, she's got friends here and no, I am not moving her to another school. I feel she needs stability right now and having her stay in this school is one way to give her that. Don't you understand that by putting her in a new school where she doesn't know anybody could be much worse for her? You people are unbelievable!"

"Mrs. Nelson, we understand your concerns. We thought it would be a way to diffuse the situation here and have Kara be in an environment with less tension."

"Oh, I see. No, Ms. Pratt, I don't think that's it at all. In fact, I'll tell you what it is. You want me to take Kara out of this school so you can wash your hands of the situation and look good to the board members. It will get rid of the situation you now have on your hands and you think it will make you get a star for the day! Well let me tell you one thing right here and right now. I will not take Kara out of the school, whether you want me to or not. That's the first thing, so don't even make as if the suggestion would be good for Kara, the only people it would be good for is you, Mr. Barton and the rest of the self-righteous morons who make up the board."

Mr. Barton stood up and spoke.

"Now, Mrs. Nelson there is no need for name-calling."

"Mr. Barton, please remember that while I am in this office I am not one of your students and you will not tell me what to do. I will say what I please, when I please, whether you agree with it or not. I will also do what is best for my daughter, no matter what YOU think I should do. Don't even think for one moment that I would hesitate to slap a lawsuit on you for everything that you have just said to me! Who do you think you are anyway? God? I'll tell you, lady, you are far from it and you want a suggestion? Keep your mouth shut or I'll find a way to shut it for you. You think I'm kidding? Just try me."

With that, Kate picked up her purse and left the office. She knew by not giving either of them time to respond, she had made an impact, the kind that left them both not knowing what to do or say next. It was perfect.

Score: Kate Nelson: 1   School: 0

CHAPTER EIGHTEEN

Kate impatiently called Ken's office and after the pleasantries with the receptionist, he answered.

"Ken Higgins"

"Mr. Higgins, this is Kate Nelson."

"Hi Kate. How are you?"

"I just got back from a meeting at my daughter's school and things didn't go all that well. I'd like to tell you about it if you have just a moment."

"Sure. Tell me what happened."

"About a week ago, I got a letter in the mail from the principal at Kara's school asking me to call and make an appointment, because there was something they wanted to discuss with me. I had no idea what it about and they wouldn't tell me until I got there."

"OK, I'm following you so far."

"I met with them earlier and I found out that the reason they asked me over there was to see if I might consider putting Kara in a different school! Can you believe they even asked me that?"

"Did they say why?"

"Yeah, they said because as the facts of the case are now known, that just having her there is too much of a disruption."

"That's ridiculous! If they have a disruptive situation on their hands, it is their job to fix it, not yours. The solution certainly isn't to take Kara out of the school. They are probably suggesting it to you because they want an easy way out; it will make their job a lot easier if you do that. I'm sure that's what they are thinking."

"I know, but can they kick Kara out of school for something like that? I've already decided I'm not taking her out. I will fight them on this. But what I'd like to know from you is can they actually do that?"

"If they did expel her from school it would have to be for a very serious reason, say having a gun on school property, something like that. The fact that they say there was an isolated "incident" isn't even close to a valid reason for them to kick her out of school."

"Oh, ok, I just wanted to make sure. By the way, Ken, I did get a little heated while at the office and told the woman in the office that she wasn't going to tell me what to do. I also said that I would say what I pleased, when I pleased."

"Good for you. Some of those people need to be straightened out every now and then. Remember they deal with children all day and they are used to treating people like that. Once in awhile, an adult needs to shake them up a bit and sounds like you did."

"I know. If someone had said what I did to them, I'd be careful how I handled this situation and that's what I want them to think. I really laid it on them. I imagine they will think twice before they suggest anything like that again."

"I'm sure. Not that I'm saying you have to bully them, but I am glad they know you are not going to take whatever they say as law. I'm glad you stood up for yourself."

"Thanks. That's usually the one thing I can do. I think I'm fairly good at it. I try to keep my temper in check most of the time, but sometimes, when it's warranted, I just let myself go. Somebody had to stand up for Kara and in this case it was me. For Pete's sake, did they forget that she is not the one causing the problem and that she is the victim here?"

"That is the problem. People like that don't think. If they did, they would have never suggested such a thing. You need to keep them under control and from what you have told me today, I think you are doing a good job of it."

"Thanks, Ken."

"You're welcome and keep me updated as to what goes on. If things escalate, and I hope they don't for your sake, I can always get another attorney to write a letter to them on your behalf and officially tell them to "back off". Believe it or not, sometimes that's all it takes to clear up a situation like this. It's amazing, but true. I have seen it happen many times before."

"Thanks for listening to me."

"You're welcome and keep me updated as to what is happening. "

"I'll do that, thanks."

Kate hung up the phone and felt better just telling Ken what went on that morning. It still bothered her that the people at the school said what they did. Kate had vowed right there and then that she wasn't going to bow down to their suggestions, wasn't going to keep quiet when they said something she didn't like and wasn't going to let them intimidate her. She had some spunk of her own and they were going to experience it firsthand if they kept on bothering her. They would eventually see that it was in their best interest to leave her and her daughter alone. If they didn't, she'd make it hard on them and enlist Ken's help with it, and that's when things might get really ugly.

Kate was going to stand her ground when it came to Kara and nobody was going to stop her; not Kara's school, not their attorney, no one.

CHAPTER NINETEEN

K ate sat in the waiting area of the jail and her thoughts on this day were no different than any other day she had been there. No matter what she had on her mind to discuss with Don, the feelings were the same. She felt eerily at ease, but still on edge just because of where she was. Kate knew from previous visits that the jail could do that to a person; have them feel fine as they approached the entrance and then all of sudden, they found themselves ill at ease, but for no apparent reason. It was an uncomfortable feeling and she experienced it each time she went to see Don. She wondered if he had that same feeling when he got here. She didn't know because now they were at the point where they didn't talk about things like that. How they felt about things was never on the agenda, like it may be for any other married couple. Theirs was now a strictly "business only" relationship; they discussed what they needed to about the house, the kids or the case and that was it. Every other subject was closed to them. Kate liked it that way; Don didn't.

He still longed to have a more personal talk with her, one where he could tell her how much he missed her and the kids and how he wished she would bring them around more. More than once she had told him she wouldn't subject them to the place and he agreed in his mind, but not his heart.

He suggested maybe they could write to him instead if they didn't want to see him in person. He waited, but no letters came. So he decided to make the first move and wrote a letter to each one of them. The boys had no interest in what he had to say and they told Kate just that. The letters to each of the twins remained unopened for days, and when they did decide to open them, they just scanned it and a few minutes later, both letters were in the trash. The boys were as different as they could be in personality, but it was surprising when they agreed with each other. Kara saw the letter from her dad and was almost scared to open it. Kate stayed close to her when she did, while Kara read it for herself:

Dear Kara,

Hi, honey! I just wanted to write a letter and tell you that even though I haven't seen you for awhile, I still love and miss you.

I hope you are doing well in school and that you are having fun in seventh grade.

Be a good girl for your mother and you can write back if you want.

I have to go now but I just wanted you to know that no matter what happens, I am still your dad and I still love you so much.
Dad

Kara's reaction to the letter was similar to Kate's, one of disinterest and boredom. She couldn't blame Kara and what did Don expect from her after everything that had happened? Kate let Kara think and feel what she wanted to, she was not about to give her the "He's Still Your Dad" speech. That might apply to other situations, but definitely not to this one. She was going to let Kara make up her own mind on how she felt about Don. She wouldn't blame Kara if she never wanted to talk to Don again and if that is what she wanted, it was fine with her.

Kate was disappointed that Don never mentioned anything about his being sorry for what he had done. She was hoping that would have been the first thing he said! But no mention of it at all, not one word. At least he could have said he was sorry for what she was having to go through, all caused by him. But no, the letter was almost "friendly", as if the criminal issue at hand didn't exist.

Kate's name was called and she followed the jail personnel and they led her to where she would be able to see and talk to Don. They brought Don out and he was happy to see her, but surprised at the same time. This was an unexpected surprise, so that made it even nicer. He sat down facing her with the glass partition separating them.

"Hi, Kate. I'm so glad to see you. This is an unexpected visit. Is everything OK at home?"

"We're doing fine, considering. I came here to discuss something else with you."

"What is it?"

"I got a letter from Kara's school the other day and they asked that I make an appointment to speak with the principal. When I got to the school, the guidance counselor also sat in on the meeting. Anyway, to make a long story short, they suggested I consider taking her out of the school! They say her being there is "a disruption" to the other students and just having her around them scares the other kids. So what do you think of that?"

"What do you think we should do? I don't want her in an environment where kids are giving her a hard time about all of this."

"I know, that was my first thought. But at the same time, it comes down to the fact that I am just not going to allow the higher-ups of the school tell me she has to leave because they don't know how to deal with it! It just makes me so mad I want to spit!"

"Calm down. I know how you get when someone annoys you."

"Calm down? Why should I calm down? All of this is easy because you don't have to deal with it on a daily basis. All you do is get up in the morning, someone brings your breakfast, you line up a few times a day for a head count, with lunch and dinner in between and that's your day. This is entirely your fault. None of this would be happening if you hadn't decided to try and abuse her in the first place. Don't you realize that?"

"Of course I do. Do you think I have no feelings at all?"

"I'm not sure what to think of you anymore. For eighteen years I thought I knew you, but apparently not. I can't even believe you would think of doing something like that to your daughter, let alone act on it. Or I should say try and act on it. I only thank God she told someone. I couldn't live with the fact if she had let it go on for who knows how long!"

"Ya know, in case you hadn't noticed, I am sitting in jail and I am kind of limited as to what I can do. Should I tell them to let me out because my wife can't handle things at home without me?"

"Don't get smug with me. If you keep it up with your attitude, I swear I will walk out of here right now and never come back!"

"No, I'm sorry, don't do that. I just get a little frustrated in here, too, you know."

"I know and even though I hate the thought of what you tried to do to Kara, it hurts me to see you in here, even though you might think otherwise. The case aside for a moment, we still have three kids to take care of. They are what is important here, nothing else."

"You're right, as always. What do you think we should do?"

"I called Ken Higgins and told him about it. He said to keep him updated and if things started to get any worse to let him know and he would send them a letter. He said sometimes that's all it takes to get them to stop."

"That was good thinking on your part. Call him if you have to."

"I will. I know that legally it might be a conflict of interest for him to help out on his own, but he is so nice, that he told me if I needed something done, one of his lawyer buddies could help. I just wanted to come down here and let you know what was happening because I think you should know. At the same time, I don't want you reading any more into it than there is. I came down here to tell you about the meeting at the school, nothing more. Things between us haven't changed."

"I figured that, I was just hoping that things might turn around for us if we present a united front to the school, well, as much as I can from here."

"I know and I appreciate that but I wanted to make sure you didn't get the wrong idea about my being here."

"I understand. I wish things were different between us but I am not going to push you."

"You ought to know by now that it won't do you any good."

"I know. You've had that stubborn streak since I met you and I just accept it."

"I am leaving now to get home before the kids do and if anything else happens that you need to know, I will see you are told, either by the attorney or by me. In the meantime, I am going to try and make sense of all of this."

"Kate, you know I want the best for you and the kids. I really do."

"I know, but you're in this place because you have a funny way of showing it. I guess you were hoping no one would find out. But now that they have, you have to put yourself in our shoes, too. Do you really expect us to feel any differently than we do in light of everything that has happened lately?"

"I guess not."

"You guess not? That's all you have to say? I was hoping for more than that from you. I'll let the kids know I saw you, whether they care or not."

With that, Kate got up to leave and Don watched her go through the door. It felt as if another chapter of his life had just ended, and that chapter came with a swift blow to the stomach. He could see the imaginary door closing on his relationship with Kate, but he was at a loss as to how to stop it. The woman he'd loved for eighteen years was slipping away from him and there was nothing he could do about it. He wanted to crawl into a hole and die. Then he remembered he was already there.

CHAPTER TWENTY

Kate was sitting at the kitchen table sipping hot coffee, when the phone rang.

"Hello?"

"Kate, it's Lori."

"Hi. It's feels like ages since we've talked but everything here has been so crazy lately. I am trying to take care of everything and some days, I feel like I am a one woman whirlwind. Other days, it's not as bad."

"That's why I was calling, to see how you are doing with all that is going on. I thought you and the kids might want to take a drive up here sometime, just to get a change of scenery. I'm sure spending time somewhere else could only do you some good."

"I'm sure you're right but for now, I just want to stay here. I like being close to the courthouse, the lawyer's office and to home, it is my one solace in all of this. That way, if I get a call from the lawyer that something new is happening with the case, I am able to drop everything and take care of it. I would be miserable if I needed to take care of something and then had to spend the time getting back here. That would literally drive me crazy, not like everything else so far hasn't."

"I know, and that's why I called. I'm worried about you, I think you're trying to do too much by yourself. Do you want me to come down there for a few days? I can cook, clean and take care of the kids. It would give you a chance to relax and if you needed to be elsewhere, you could just go. I don't mind, really. I want to help you."

"I know, and I appreciate it so much. I think the four of us are handling it pretty well so far on our own. If you were here, I would feel like I had to entertain you and with the way things are, I don't know if I could do that. "

"Kate, that's ridiculous and you know it."

"Maybe, but that's the way I feel. I think that I'm harried some days, but for the most part, the kids and I are hanging in there. I feel more at ease with just them and me at the moment. I want to show them that despite what is happening with their father, I am handling it and this is how it is going to be from now on."

"I suppose you're right, but I'm worried about you."

"Don't be, I'm fine. Well, relatively fine. If some day you call and I don't answer the home phone or the cell phone, then start to worry! That's when I'll need you to check up on me."

"You know I am always just a phone call away."

"I know and you've been great about keeping in touch. I love you for it. Just check in with me every now and then. In the meantime, we're fine."

"OK. I'm proud of you for taking all of this on yourself and you are really showing the kids how strong you've been through all of this. Just let me know if you need anything."

"I will and thanks for checking in with me. I don't mean to ignore you it's just that with everything that's going on, you can get lost it in sometimes."

"I know, I understand."

"Thanks for everything. Sometimes just talking to you settles me down."

"I'm here anytime for you, Kate. You know that."

"Have to get back to my cup of coffee before it gets cold. I'll talk to you soon and thanks for the pep talk."

"I'll talk to you soon."-

"Thanks for calling, bye."

The kids had off from school and the twins had already left to hang out with their friends. She gave each of them some money for lunch and Kate knew they wouldn't be back till supper time. So, Kate would have the entire day to spend with Kara. She was looking forward to it because Kate thought it would do both of them good to spend time together without interruption from anyone or anything else. She wasn't sure how Kara would feel about it and even though she was almost a teenager, Kara still liked to hang out with Kate. Any mother would appreciate that, but Kate also knew the day was soon approaching where Kara would rather be with her friends than with her mother. So she decided she was going to take advantage of it and enjoy Kara's company while she was still willing to let her do it. Kara walking sleepily into the kitchen and Kate got up and poured her a glass of orange juice.

"What would you like for breakfast? Do you want me to cook something for you?"

"Nah.........I'm not real hungry. I'll just have the juice."

"OK, I'll sit here and finish my coffee while you finish your juice. I thought we might do something fun today, since it's just you and I. Would you like that?"

"Yeah, like what?"

"How about later on we go to the mall or to a movie?"

"Can we do both?"

Kate had to smile at Kara's suggestion. That was Kara, still the little girl at heart, always wanting the most out of the situation. But after all she had been through, if that's all Kara was asking for, how could Kate say no? Kara deserved the world, and Kate was going to try and make her happy, at least for one day. Kate told Kara to take a shower and then they'd be ready to leave. Kara agreed and didn't argue because she was ready to get on with the day's activities, too.

Kate still sat at the table sipping even more coffee and thinking what all this was doing to her daughter. Kara didn't say much about it and Kate didn't want to be the one to bring up a bad subject, but Don's case stared them in the face every hour of every day. It was like a dull ache that never went away. When she had the chance to do something alone with Kara she jumped on it because she was always trying to make Kara get her mind off the case, and Kate owed her that much. After what had happened with Don, who did Kara have now?

Kate had to be both mother and father to her and that had been hard for both of them. With the boys it had been a little easier, but it was totally different, too. First off, they were not the victims here, Kara was. The boys already had a relationship with Kate and as they grew older and spent more time away from the house, they didn't need to be with Don all the time, either. So not having Don in the house was not as big of a change for them as it was for Kara. She had always been "Daddy's Little Girl" and Kate wanted that for her daughter.

But now all of that had changed and Kate how no idea how they were going to come out of this and even if Kara would have any contact with him for the rest of her life. Kate would see to it that Kara was protected, at any price. If that meant that the boys had to forego seeing their dad, then that's the way it had to be. Kate would see to it that Kara was the one who would come out of this smelling like a rose. If Don was reduced to being the snake in the grass, then so be it. He didn't deserve any special favors and Kate's keeping Kara in Don's good graces wasn't one of them. All she owed her daughter now was love and protection and Kate would come out fighting trying to accomplish it. Even the flare-up with the school was enough to upset Kate, but she wasn't going to let it interfere with Kara's well being and security. The whole point was to keep Kara as comfortable and secure as she could be in her surroundings, so why didn't the school understand that?

They just didn't want to take the time and effort to keep the situation under control. It was easier for them to just get rid of the problem instead of dealing with it. That school was in for a rude awakening if Kate had anything to do with it. She had just begun to fight! How dare they even consider asking her to remove Kara from the only school she had ever attended! Bunch of blowhards.....she'd show them and Kate still had some fight left in her to do it, too.

Kate picked up the house phone while waiting for Kara to come downstairs and told the boys what her plans were for the day with Kara and that if they needed her, they could reach her on the cell phone. That was Kate, always making sure she had everything covered and always making sure the kids were fine. If they were away from her, she wanted them to know she could be easily reached and they could call her and she would come running.

Kara came down the stairs and told Kate she was ready. Kate picked up her purse and car keys and headed out the door. Hurray for some time away from the phone, the mailbox and most of all, the reminders of Don that were everywhere in the house. It was almost as if a death had occurred, similar to when you see clothes of the recently deceased hanging in the closet, their shoes neatly lined up on the floor, etc. Its eerie memories haunt you for months to come without your realizing it. Your inner strength is tested to the limit, but this situation was different.

It wasn't the death of a person, it was the death of a lifestyle and Kate knew it was up to her to pick up the pieces of their former family life and start all over. She was going to try but nobody said it was going to be easy and so far, it hadn't been.

CHAPTER TWENTY-ONE

D on just wiled away the days sleeping, showing up for head counts at the specified times, watching the time go by while out in the yard and counting down the minutes till they could come back in again. He spent most of each day resting on his cot staring at the ceiling. He had no interest in visiting the jail library or doing anything productive. Lazy was the order of the day.

At first, he had hoped they would offer him the chance to be part of a road gang, where each day worked equaled a day off the time left he had to serve. But now he even had no interest in that, either. He was at the lowest point of his life and almost didn't care whether he lived or died, with the one exception that he always wanted to know how Kate and the kids were. Even though he was stuck in jail, and the nature of the crime he was charged with was unforgivable, that was always what he wanted to know. He would spend his days thinking of ways to find out what was going on at home.

He tried to send letters to the kids in hopes of having them send him a letter back, but that hadn't happened and deep down, he knew he couldn't blame them. Whenever he got mail, it was from his attorney keeping him up to date on the case. It was never what he hoped for – a letter from the family and he knew it never would be unless he could prove himself innocent of the charges. Even then, there would be no assurance of Kate and the kids having respect for him again. This whole thing had irrevocably damaged that part of their lives, never to be reactivated again. He knew he was hoping against hope, but it was all he had, and that wasn't much. This was a low point for him and he wondered how he was going to continue to cope.

There was no bright spot to shoot for, no light at the end of the tunnel and no expectation of anything different happening. His hopes had been dashed and his dream that the nightmare be over was not reality; it was wishful thinking, the kind that was so unrealistic that it made no sense. The worst of all was that he knew it, deep inside of him he knew that they were pipe dreams, never with a chance in hell of ever happening. His knowledge of what had transpired so far in the case made it impossible to think otherwise. He knew he was stuck in jail for the next 29 months and there was no getting around it. The best thing he could do for himself now was just make the best of it, bide his time, stay out of trouble and pray for the day he got to walk out of here. It was the only thing he could think about, the only thing he worried about. He worried about how people would treat him when he did get out. That was so far in the future it wasn't even worth thinking about. The things that bothered him now were the things he had no control over and those were the things he had difficulty with. He wondered if a lot of the inmates had those same kind of thoughts and if they worried what kind of life they would eventually have on the outside. That was his recurring dream; he called it his own personal boomerang effect, because no matter how he tried to get rid of them, those very same thoughts kept on coming back to haunt him.

He spent his time daydreaming of what he wanted to happen rather than what was most likely going to happen, and he didn't want to face it right now. He knew things were going to go from bad to worse for him and there was nothing he could do to stop that speeding locomotive that was just a few seconds away from killing him. That's how he felt lately and like a song that gets in your head and replays itself constantly to the point where you are tempted to hit yourself with a hammer to stop it, he was trying to brace himself for the inevitable. Don was looking for new ways to deal with his ever fading influence on his family. It was if he could close his eyes at night and see images of Kate and the kids slipping through his fingers, to be lost forever. Of course, that was not what he wanted, but things kept pointing to that result. It was similar to the feeling of being lost in a raging snowstorm as you approached a mountain with a huge avalanche just about to bury you. You hate what is going to momentarily happen, you fear it, you lose it and then you just succumb.

It was like that for Don every minute of every day. He couldn't escape the thoughts that everything he loved and cherished was slowly being taken away from him. Jail was not the place where you could take care of things on your own, you ate when someone said it was time to, you showered when they told you to and if the officials had the ability to tell you what to think and when to think it, they would have. This was the kind of world Don was in now. Everything else was skewed, like looking through a lens where all the images are out of focus and you feel like a kid in the house of mirrors. When he did manage to snap back to reality, the news wasn't all that good there, either. Kate's visits to the jail were so sparse and irregular that at any given moment he could count them on one hand. There was absolutely no word from the kids, either by letter or through Kate. He agreed with Kate that it wasn't right to force them to be in contact with him, yet how do you just stop suddenly having contact with the people you love most in the world? That was very hard for Don and he was constantly struggling with it. It made no sense for him to demand such contact because that would never work if the kids had no desire to do so, which was apparently the case. He tried to put it out of his mind and just leave it alone for awhile. Sometimes you could "think something to death" and that's what was happening to him. It needed time to settle and that was probably best for all of them right now with the charges and the case itself being so new. Plus, he had to make himself understand that all of this was new to Kate and the kids. His days were full of the basics: he ate, slept, read, watched a little TV and had an hour each day outside. That's it. Nothing ever changed with his schedule. He existed and did what he could to sustain his life, but that's all. Never any extras, never any change of plans, never anything else. The rules were adhered to and the boredom of it all played out each and every day. You could set your watch by it. If you were in that jail, you lived a life of simplicity with no changes in schedule, ever. You could wish it, you could will it, you could even demand it, but it didn't matter, the rules were set, the rules were followed and that was it.

He was living in a world where he knew now what he would be doing next week at the same time because nothing ever changed. It was called living in an institution; everything on schedule and everything done at the same time as yesterday. There were never any changes and there was never any time allowed for creativity in the schedule. The old saying "written in stone" must be the jail motto.

Before his arrest, Don was an avid reader and spent many weekends in the backyard reading the latest murder mystery or whatever else appealed to him at the local library. When the kids were young, he took them there quite often and let them check out books of their own choosing, while he browsed the shelves for himself. He never thought of it as a big deal, mostly he was trying to get the kids interested in reading. Teachers had been telling him for years that one of the best things to do was to read to a child when they were very young and then let them watch you read. That way, they would understand that reading was important. Even now, while in jail, he was able to use the library there but he had no interest in it. Maybe he would later on, but for now all he wanted and all he could think of was what was going to happen to his family. He understood that things would be changed forever between them, but that didn't mean that he had to like it. He could like it, he could hate it, but whatever was destined to happen, he just couldn't change it and that is what bothered him most. He was stuck in this crappy place and had an attitude to match.

Deep down, he knew that Kate was going to try and keep the kids as far away from him as she could. He couldn't really blame her, he didn't want them coming to the jail, it wasn't a good place for them to be. Yet, he had such a longing to see them. He didn't have a leg to stand on when it came to Kate's telling him how she planned to handle the issue of the kids. If he gave her an argument about it, all she had to do was tell him that the boys were at an age where they could decide for themselves and he had to admit, she was right about that. As for Kara, since she was the alleged victim in the case, no judge in his right mind was going to allow him to be near her. It was stories like that that killed guys in jail. No wonder the suicide rate among inmates was so high. When family members told them stuff like that, what else was left for them to do? All Don knew now was that the world was starting to royally suck, as it never had before, and he wanted no part of it. Up till now, his way of dealing with it was to go to sleep and block it out of his mind. The only flaw in that logic was that when he woke up, he realized that nothing had changed and the same scenario played over again in his mind. From where he sat, he had no ability to fix anything, no ability to get to the resources needed to fix them, mostly he needed to be around Kate and tell her that he would do anything to stay in her good graces. He knew it was futile, but what else did he have going for him? He was a tortured man, but the worst of it came from him. He was a man who was destined for a future of loneliness and despair and that was now his lot in life and he had to prepare himself for it. His attorney had basically told him the same thing; it was unfortunate but true. Don even sunk so low as to ask his attorney to intervene on his behalf with Kate. As he sat in his cell, he couldn't even believe he actually did it. That was insane but at the time, he had to feel as if he was actually taking some action on his own to go ahead and try to smooth things over with her. He knew it would do no good, but he wanted the satisfaction of feeling like he did something, anything. It was stupid and irreversible and now he felt ashamed and embarrassed about what he had done. There was nothing he could do to erase what had happened, he just had to live with it. He was doomed, plain and simple.

He was as sad as a man could be and it was heart wrenching to see it happening before Kate's very eyes. The man she knew as her husband had always been so vibrant, smart and handsome and she was so proud to be at his side. But now that same man was losing control of his emotions and his spirit. He was spiraling downward and as he did, it was going to be a hard climb back. Although in jail, he seemed to be lost and not able to concentrate on anything. He had no interest in doing anything but sitting quietly in his cell. He didn't want to read, write, watch television or take part in any of the things he was actually allowed to do. All he wanted to do was think and when he wasn't thinking, he was sleeping. Those were his only two activities and for now, he liked it that way. That's how he wanted to spend his time while in jail, so Kate didn't have much to say about it. She tried to put herself in his shoes, but she couldn't imagine ever abusing one of their children, either. That fact stopped her short of thinking any further about how Don felt. She had no sympathy for him, he had put himself in this place and he deserved to be punished. Kate knew he was suffering, not the physical kind, but the mental kind, which can invade and tear apart your very soul. That's the part of him that needed forgiveness. She didn't know where that was going to come from, she just knew it wasn't coming from her. She had no intention of forgiving him for what he tried to do to their daughter. The fact that he would have let that scenario play out made her sick. Who knows how long it might have gone on if she hadn't found out. She looked at her hands now and they were cold and sweaty. Yet they had the appearance of strength to them, too. Hands that could do some damage if they had to and if they wanted to. They were hands that could most likely hurt someone when called upon to do so. Like the fact that she could easily have placed those very hands around Don's neck and squeezed the life out of him for what he had tried to do to their daughter. She was angry and she was hurt but her mission now was to make sure he was the one who was angry and hurt.

Kate was sure he was angry about the fact that there didn't seem to be much hope of Don's getting out of jail anytime soon. He was hurt because he had moments of guilt for what he had let himself do.

Kate could now say to herself, "Mission Accomplished."

CHAPTER TWENTY-TWO

Kate pulled into the driveway with Kara sitting on the passenger side, trying to balance two hot pizzas on her lap. She told Kara to stay there for a minute while she went inside and told the boys to come out and each carry one into the house. Kate had called the twins earlier to let them know of the dinner plans and they were thrilled about it. Tommy said, "Thanks, mom, you're so great." Kate felt good that he was happy but actually she had done it more for herself. She was in no mood to cook and clean up tonight because after a day at the mall and movies with Kara, she was just too tired for anything more taxing than takeout. This was the perfect solution and whenever she planned pizza for dinner, all the kids were happy. Kate was happy too because it made for a quick and easy cleanup, too. It was a good way to start off the evening.

After dinner's cleanup, the kids went to their rooms for homework and television watching. Kate sat on the couch trying to collect her thoughts. She grabbed the stack of mail and separated it into piles of what to throw away and what to look at. Among the assorted shapes and colors of envelopes she saw one that piqued her attention and there is was: a letter from Kara's school. Kate's first reaction was, "Oh no, not again!" Sure enough, there was the envelope staring straight back at her and she hesitated a moment before opening it. It reminded her of that childhood toy when you would open a can and a snake would pop out and make you scream with surprise. This letter didn't have a snake inside, Kate thought, probably just a snake who wrote it. She remembered how condescending all the school officials were that day she had the meeting with them. They all thought they were really something. In reality, most of them were a bunch of two bit losers who stuck together because none of them had any people skills or effective way of communicating a problem, so no wonder they were one big happy family. Kate was about to bust up this unlikely family reunion on her own this time. They'd better not be thinking of giving her any more trouble about it. She was ready for them this time. Last time around, she was taken back because she hadn't expected it. She wasn't going to put herself in that position anymore and she, like they say, would be armed and dangerous, at least on paper. They might have tried to pull stuff like this on other parents, but they weren't going to do it to her. If the other parents didn't stand up to them, that was their problem. She wasn't them, nor did she want to be. She wasn't going to cower down to any of them, and they didn't know what they were going to start if they tried any smart stuff with her or her daughter. Let them just try it, she thought. OK, she braced herself and tore the end of the envelope enough to pull out the letter inside. Again, it started with the words:

Dear Mr. and Mrs. Nelson:

She knew the school was addressing that letter because they were both Kara's parents and even with Don in jail, that didn't change the fact. But as the weeks and months started to go by, she was getting used to handling things on her own and to see a letter addressed like that both startled and annoyed her. She had a feeling she might need to keep Ken's number on speed dial, but at the same time, she didn't want to annoy him. Although she would absolutely not let the school make a fool of her, either. They didn't realize who they were trying to start a fight with. If that's what they wanted, that's what they were going to get. She wasn't going to back down and even before she started to read the letter, she started to get angry.

Dear Mr. and Mrs. Nelson:
 Not long ago, we met at the school office to discuss the situation

*with your daughter and the trouble it was causing here. Since that
meeting, we had hoped things would calm down but we are finding just
the opposite to be true. Students are making rude comments, not only
to your daughter, but to teachers as well. Those teachers are reporting
what is going on to me so I can rectify it. However, at this point, I
have not been successful in trying to manage an effective way to stop
it completely.*

*Unfortunately, kids can be cruel, and as educators, we cannot fol-
low them around constantly to make sure they act the way we want
them to.*

*Therefore, in light of the situation, we feel it may be best to have
Kara attend another school, perhaps where the situation is not so volatile and where the situation with her father is not as well known as it
is here. We enjoy having Kara as a student in our school but we feel her
well-being is at stake as long as she is here.*

*As you know, we are a private school and we have the right to
suggest the student be placed elsewhere when problems arise. Although
we know none of this is Kara's doing, we feel we cannot have this situation go on.*

*Please consider placement at another school and in the meantime,
if you would like to discuss it further with either myself or other school
personnel, please let us know.*
Thank you.
Sincerely,

Michael C. Barton, Principal

If the man was here now, I would wring his neck! Is he kidding me?
Oh, wait till I get my hands on him! Kate was so mad she couldn't see
straight. What should she do? In the old days, when something like this
came up, it was run to Don. These days, that option was gone so it was
up to her to make the decision. She planned to give Ken Higgins a call

in the morning and hash it out with him. You want a fight, Mr. School Principal? OK, great, I'll see that you get one!

"Good morning, Mr. Higgins' office."

"Yes, good morning. Is Mr. Higgins in please?"

"Let me check for you. Your name, please?"

"This is Kate Nelson. Actually, Mr. Higgins represents my husband, Donald Nelson, in a criminal case. However, I need to talk to him about an issue that is going on at my daughter's school."

"Thank you. Hold on please."

Kate was starting to feel an ache in her back and a pain at the base of her neck. She took her left hand and starting rubbing her neck, as she waited for the attorney to get on the line.

"This is Ken Higgins speaking. How can I help you?"

"Hi, this is Kate Nelson. I was wondering if you could help me with something."

"Sure, if I can. What is it?"

"I just got another letter from Kara's school and they are suggesting I take her out of the school because they say that her being there is causing a problem due to Don's case. She's been in that school since she started kindergarten! All her friends are there! With the thing with Don, I was trying to keep everything the same for the kids. They already have too much to deal with, let alone having to go to a new school! I don't know what to do."

"First off, calm down. Don't let them frazzle you. That's exactly what they are trying to do in the hopes you will bow down to them and decide to put Kara somewhere else. Then you have made it easy for them, they get what they want.

I have a suggestion and tell me what you think about it."

"OK."

"What if I draft a letter to the school saying that we insist they let Kara stay there? From being in this field as long as I have, I have found that sometimes that's all it takes to clear up a situation like this. Of

course, I will hint at the fact that we will sue if they don't stop sending you letters like this and if they keep telling you to remove your
daughter from the school."

"Really? You think it will work?"

"We won't know till we try it, but I think it's a good strategy at
this point."

"Let's do it. Can you just add the cost onto the bill for Don's
case?"

"Sure. It's not going to be that much, around $150.00 or so but
here's hoping it's going to be well worth it in the long run."

"I hope so. I really don't need this right now, along with everything
else that is going on."

"I know. It's unfortunate that the school is leaning on you that
way, but I have a feeling they may change their mind once they get the
letter. Of course, I will mail you a copy before sending it so you can
approve it before it goes out."

"That will be great, thank you."

"You're welcome. I'll get right on it because I know you'd like to
get this settled soon."

"You're right about that! Thanks again."

"It's fine. You should get the copy of the letter in a few days."

Kate ran her hand through her blonde streaked hair and was enjoying the sense of relief she felt after just talking to Ken. Lawyers usually
get a bad rap, but she thought about the fact that they were the ones
people turned to when they were in trouble. Like any other profes-
sion, there were good and bad ones and maybe theirs was a good one.
She couldn't rely on that because only time would tell. Ken had a great
way with his clients and he always tried to reassure her that things
would be ok. He seemed to understand what she was going through.
Kate always felt like she could honestly talk to him about the case and
he never gave her the feeling that she was stupid for bringing it up.
That made him worth what they were paying him. He gave her a sense

of calm and she liked that about him. Even now, with this stuff from Kara's school, here she was at her wit's end and he politely told her he would draft a letter to them and that might be the end of it. She would be eternally grateful to him if it was!

Kate was tempted to call Kara's school and tell them what they could do with their damn letter. But then after thinking about it, decided it would be better if she left it alone and had them be surprised when they got the letter from the law firm. She would have given anything to be in the office when the principal read it, just to see his reaction.

Kate thought it may be as Ken said, "it may just all work itself out." Kate was anxious to see if it would.

CHAPTER TWENTY-THREE

Kate hurriedly opened the letter from the law firm and wanted to see what it said. She wondered what else they would have added that she couldn't have said to the principal in person. She reached in for the letter, unfolded it and started to read:

Dear Mr. Barton:

My name is Ken Higgins and I represent Donald and Kate Nelson, parents of Kara Nelson, who is currently a student at your school. I know that you are aware of the situation with Kara's father, Donald Nelson. It has come to my attention that you sent Mr. and Mrs. Nelson a letter suggesting that they consider removing their daughter from the school (see enclosed copy).

I am aware of the fact that you asked my clients to consider removing their daughter from the school, which they have no intention of doing. Secondly, you are in violation of the law by asking them to remove their child when that child has done nothing wrong.

I also know that Kara is not in violation of any of the school requirements for expulsion, and that if you did try and expel her now, you would have no basis on which to do so. Therefore, even though you may wish Kara to be removed from the school, your expulsion of her would only lead to much bigger problems for you. Please be advised that if you do expel Kara, without cause, my clients are prepared to file a lawsuit against you, which you will undoubtedly lose.

We hope to resolve this situation amicably before it reaches the litigation stage.

Please do not contact my clients further. Any correspondence con-

cerning this matter should be addressed directly to my office.

I await your prompt reply.

Sincerely,

Ken Higgins, Esq.

Kate was impressed with the tone of the letter. It was polite, yet firm. It spelled out exactly what she wanted to say, but Ken said it better. She wondered if this letter alone would be enough to convince the school officials not to pursue the matter any further. Ken had already told her that Kara had not done anything to warrant an expulsion, so the school couldn't legally do that. Kate worried that they may hound her to death in the meantime and make it so bad for her that she would have to put Kara in another school just to escape the aggravation. However, after reading the draft of the letter, she felt a lot better.

She picked up the phone and dialed Ken's office number. She asked that his secretary relay to him the message that the letter was fine and to go ahead and send it to the school. She said she would give him the message, and as soon as they heard something from the school, they would let her know.

She sat down on the sofa and turned on the television. She really didn't care what was on, she just needed something to take her mind off of everything that was happening. Any type of diversion was welcome at this point. After watching the evening news, she turned off the television and the lights and went to bed. She'd know soon enough what the school thought of it and for that, she'd just have to wait.

Kate was glad that she could rely on her part-time job to keep her occupied. Before Don's arrest, she worked full-time but that was impossible now. Taking care of the paperwork with Don's case was nearly a full-time job itself. Lately, she had been receiving paperwork from all kinds of women's groups asking her not to drop the charges against Don. Of course, she had no intention of doing so and it was amazing that a case like Don's would warrant these people trying to contact her. Did groups such as those have a database they could research and just get information on how to contact her? Otherwise, how would they have found her? She hadn't responded to them as of yet and she thought she might do so because theirs was a good cause and she liked the fact that women's groups would band together like that. It gave her a feeling of solidarity that other women supported the situation she was in without even knowing her. It helped to keep busy and of course, now there was a real need to make money with three kids to support. She and Don had adequate savings but she knew she didn't want to get into a situation where there was no money to fall back on. Don had always made a good living and it had been an adjustment for Kate to live on only one income. Each time she saw Don, he told her to make it easy on herself and use the money from the savings account. She thought of the money in that account as something she would use as a last resort. For now, she was trying to concentrate on doing what she could to support the family. It seemed as if every time she turned around, there was some little incidental expense to take care of.

The kids needed money for field trips, special workbooks to co-incide with their courses of study and the like. Besides that, the kids wanted to go to the movies with their friends and she wasn't going to tell them no. They needed all the attention and love she could give them now that she was the only one they could depend on. She felt sorry for them in that way. She never wanted them to be in the situation they found themselves in, through no fault of their own. They were good kids, all of them, and they didn't deserve this. It was amazing to think that when Don decided to commit the unthinkable crime he was accused of, the consequences of that action had far reaching effects. It reminded her of what happened when you threw a stone into a calm lake and you watched it form ever larger ripples from where it originally hit the water. They were the ones who had to keep those ripples from getting ever larger and spinning out of control. It was

Don who had changed all of their lives dramatically and unfortunately, they were the ones who had to live with it now. They were the ones who had to endure the stares, the whispers and the pointing of fingers. They were the ones who had to keep their heads up high when some-one snubbed them. Why couldn't all those people remember that they weren't the ones on trial here, Don was. When all of this started, she had promised to do her best for the four of them. Making that promise was the easy part, keeping it was the hard part.

CHAPTER TWENTY-FOUR

Dear Mr. Higgins:

I am in receipt of your letter concerning the situation with one of our students, Miss Kara Nelson.

After reviewing the contents of the letter with my staff and the school board, please be advised that the school will not be taking any further action in this matter and Ms. Nelson may remain a student at the school without any further intrusion from the board.

We thank you for alerting us to the possible legal consequences had the school initiated any action against Ms. Nelson or her family. We trust this decision to be the best for all parties.

If you have any other questions, please do not hesitate to contact my office.

Thank you.

Sincerely,

Michael Barton, Principal

Well, well, Mr. Higgins, you earned your money this time around. Kate found it amazing that a letter from Ken was all it took to get the people at the school to back down. She was lucky she had hired Ken when she heard what he suggested they do and it had such a great outcome. People complain about lawyers all the time and the exorbitant fees they charge, but if this was the kind of success they could get for their clients, they would almost be justified in what they charge.

After reading the letter, Kate felt so relieved; it was one more problem she didn't have to deal with. She immediately called Ken's office and told him how happy she was with the results. He said he was glad it had turned out the way it did and that he doubted there would be anything further and as they say in court, "case closed". She hoped he was right. The nerve of those people at the school thinking she would take their crap! What if she had done what the school suggested and put the burden on Kara, making her feel insecure in a new place?

Kate wanted Kara to feel secure because she was already dealing with more than someone her age should have to. Kate didn't want to move her from the school she loved, but Kate did doubt if the school would be able to handle the situation. She thought the best course of action would be to keep Kara at the school, but Kate would have to monitor what was going on there a lot more closely than she had been doing. For the moment, things seemed to be calm on the school front and she hoped it stayed that way. She would be glad when Kara was out of that school in another year and would be starting high school. Maybe by then, publicity in Don's case would have died down. She was hoping that was the case because she wanted Kara to be able to focus on her studies and other school related activities. She didn't want Don's case to overshadow everything Kara did. By then, she hoped the kids who had been mean to her because of Don would be into something or someone else. Her daughter didn't need the taunts or nasty remarks from the kids who had made them in the past. Sometimes Kate wished she could just take those kids by the collar and choke them and have them realize who they were dealing with. But she knew she couldn't for two reasons: first, they were kids and second, she didn't know who they were and Kara wouldn't tell her. She wasn't going to press Kara about it unless the situation got out of hand.

For now, things were at an unsteady calm, and Kate realized that things could blow up at any second, but if that happened, she'd be ready. Thank goodness for Ken Higgins, he had been great on this one. His expertise had saved them so much heartache. His job with Don had been a lot more intense, but at least he did get him the plea offer, which was so much better than sitting through a lengthy trial. Kate weighed the advantages of having him as their lawyer and even though his fees weren't cheap, she had to admit that he had a good job for them so far. Actually, once Don accepted the plea offer, there really wasn't much more for Ken to do. Ken completed the necessary paperwork and filed it with the court. With Don's signature on the document, the plea offer, and Don's acceptance of it, was official. The physical work of the case was now over, but the long lasting effects never would be.

It could never be said that Don hadn't caused all of them hours and hours of sadness and heartache. Thanks to Don, her children were all of a sudden thrown into a world where they saw life's nasty side firsthand. They saw life as they once knew it immediately disappear and as hard as she tried to keep life normal for them, there was no way she could do that. Tommy and Timmy took on the new role as Kara's protectors, making sure one of them was either with her or not far from her. Kate didn't want the boys to feel as if they had to monitor Kara's every move, but they told Kate they didn't mind, and that they wanted to.

Tommy, the more vocal of the twins, once told Kate, "Just let anybody come near her and try to bother her and I'll flatten him." Kate was proud of him for wanting to protect his little sister, but she didn't want him to feel pressure that all of a sudden it was his job to step into Don's shoes. After all, he wasn't yet an adult and Kate had no intention of letting him take on all that responsibility. She had no problem with Tommy watching out for her, but she didn't want him to feel as if it was his job, 24 hours a day. She and Tommy always had a good relationship and she could talk to him. He was very approachable and for that, she was thankful.

Timmy, on the other hand, was quiet and he spent his time thinking about things before he took any action. It was more his style to just "lie in wait" rather than jump right in before he had all the facts. However, all Tommy had to do was to say something, and Timmy was right there beside him. They looked alike, but underneath, they were like night and day. Ever since they were little, Kate worried about them having their own personality and not being too dependent on the other. That's why she refused to dress them alike. She wanted each of them to realize that although they were twins, each was their own person and it seemed that she had succeeded in having them think and act for themselves. She was grateful for that and the last thing she wanted was although carbon copies of each other in looks, they were very much individuals, as any brothers who weren't twins would be.

As it stood now, Don was in jail for the length of the plea offer. He wasn't going anywhere for a long time and with Kate's decision not to visit him and concentrate on her and the kids, things with Don were pretty much at a standstill, which after all that had happened, is exactly where she wanted them. She knew she was going to have to make a decision about her future and if she wanted the marriage to continue. With everything else that had happened, she wasn't ready to make that decision yet. That time was getting ever closer; she just didn't want to face it right now. Don wasn't going anywhere, so there was time. Thinking if she wanted to get a divorce or not was never something she thought she would have to face, and she dreaded it, for whatever reason, whether necessary or not. She also thought she would have never had to deal with a situation that involved a criminal case against Don and that Kara would be the victim. It just proved that when you thought your life was in order and things were going along fine, everything could change in a moment's notice and when they did, you needed to be ready. Life can catch you off guard sometimes and its how you choose to deal with it that makes the difference.

For years, they were the perfect little family; twin boys and a daughter. Who could ask for more? Plus, all of them were adorable with their streaked hair from the Florida sun, blue eyes and freckles.

Any one of the three could have been on a tv commercial where it asked for the actor to be "an All-American" kid. They looked like the kids next door and that's exactly who they were until Don was arrested. After that, everything changed.

The kids were still the same, it was everyone else who changed. They were treated differently by those who knew them, with very few exceptions. Friends of theirs all of sudden weren't around much. They told the kids they were busy, had homework, etc. but Kate knew better. She was sure it was the parents of the kids' friends that were making all of this happen. They were the ones who were all of sudden shaken up and didn't want to let their kids associate with any of the three of them. Was having a father who was in jail a disease? Was it something to be avoided at all costs? It put the kids in a weird position and Kate felt sorry for them because they didn't understand it. In time, they would realize the magnitude of it all, but at the moment it was difficult for them. Kate wished she could shield them from everything evil in the world, but that was wishful thinking on her part.

Tommy and Timmy knew they were going to have to shoulder more of the responsibility around the house now that Don would be gone for an extended period of time. So far, they had been good about it and Kate tried not to load them up with too many chores. They were busy with their studies and after school activities so she didn't want to jam them up with lots of other stuff during the little free time they did have. At the same time, she wanted to make sure that they knew all four of them were a team and they were going to have to carry the load without Don. So far, they were doing well with that and Kate found that she could depend on her two sons, and that was a good feeling.

Kate knew her kids, but when it came to Don, did she know herself? How do you will yourself to stop loving a person after eighteen years? You have the police arrest him for a crime against your daughter and all the heartache with that will take care of it. It makes it easy to take the love away. Then you decide what happens to the relationship.

That might have been the hardest decision in all of this and Kate decided it was time for another phone call to the attorney.

She felt as if she was single handedly keeping him in business. It was amazing how complicated their lives had become in such a short time but complicated or not, Kate was working her way toward the end result she wanted.

CHAPTER TWENTY-FIVE

Don was lying on the bunk in his cell, listlessly looking at a magazine he didn't care about. It passed the time and that's all. His thoughts were always on the same subject: Kate. He was in a no win situation with her. She rarely visited him and when she did, it was generally for a purpose and not just a friendly visit. On those occasions, she took care of what she came to discuss with him and left. No extra time spent, no nice words, just business and then she was gone. He never had a chance to actually spend time with her to discuss their relationship; whatever was left of it. It put him in a habitually foul mood just thinking about it. He realized he was turning into one of those other inmates he noticed when he first got here.

He only did what he had to do. He didn't even volunteer to be a part of the group of inmates who worked in the community to have time taken off his sentence. Maybe he would later on, but right now he couldn't handle much more than doing the bare minimum.

It was a huge effort just for him to keep himself well groomed. The last time Kate saw him he was sporting unruly stubble on his face and he looked like he hadn't showered in days. This wasn't the Don she knew, but in light of all that had happened, could she really expect him to be? It was hard for both of them now; he had no motivation to keep himself clean and well. He felt he had lost everything dear to him and figured there was no use in trying. It made no difference to him now. He was a lost soul, one who just followed the crowd of inmates when it was time for a headcount and that's about all he could manage.

After Kate had seen him like this a number of times, she wondered if she should call Ken and discuss it with him. She didn't want to appear like she cared and she had to remember that Ken was Don's attorney, not his social worker.

If Don wanted to stay in the depths of despair, then let him. It wasn't her job to pull him out of it, either. He had a lot to deal with and she was sure he was hurting, but she was too. She tried not to show it openly to the kids, but she was sure they knew she had a lot to take care of. She was wearing a lot of hats, including being both mother and father to the kids. She wasn't about to add Don's bad attitude and laziness to the list. Deep down she hated to admit to herself that she really didn't care. That thought alone gave her some freedom of knowing it was up to her to take of everything on the home front.

Yet she knew that no matter what, he was still her husband and that's where the anxiety was for her. It would have been easy for Kate to support him if he had committed a crime against another person. Being that his victim was their own daughter made it impossible for Kate to stand behind him through all of this. No one could blame her for the way she felt, it was a strange position for her to be in.

It was a choice between Don and Kara and she chose Kara, and Don would have to learn to deal with it. He knew that's what it would come down to and that she would choose Kara. He would want her to, but that left him alone with not one person to lean on. Kate felt when presented with the facts, he didn't deserve to have anyone on his side. What he did, or tried to do, was despicable and he deserved the mess he was in.

There would be no more going out to lunch at a nice restaurant with the kids on Sundays after church. There would be no PTA meetings at the kids' school. There would be no more chaperoning the kids' field trips. There was no turning back, his former life as he knew it was over. He knew it and so did Kate, he just couldn't admit it to himself. It was so depressing for him and some days he just could not deal with it.

Sleep was his only escape and when sleep did come to him, he was glad; it was the only respite he got from the tragedy he was living. Some nights it got so bad he prayed he would die. He really didn't want to end his life. He couldn't see much point in going on the way he was, but he was too much of a coward to end his life. The jail chaplain had unexpectedly come to visit him one afternoon. At first, he resisted and didn't want to talk to him, but after the chaplain spoke, Don started to open up to him. He kept going over the conversation in his mind.

"Hello, Mr. Nelson. I'm Chaplain Jenkins and I wanted to stop by and introduce myself. I try to make the rounds and visit the inmates from time to time. I haven't had the opportunity to meet you before this. Would now be a good time to talk with you for a few minutes?"

Don answered with, "Yeah, sure."

Don really had no desire to talk to him, but didn't want to be rude. He continued to listen to what Chaplain Jenkins had to say.

"First off, I am not here to preach to you or to discuss why you are here. I do want you to know that I am available to talk to you whenever you feel the need."

Don answered with a feeble, "OK."

"So, tell me Mr. Nelson, do you have a family?"

"Yes, I've been married to my wife, Kate, for eighteen years and I have 17 year old twin sons, Timmy and Tommy, and a 12 year old daughter, Kara."

"That sounds like a lovely family. You should be very proud."

"Well, I used to be, I'm not sure what I feel about anything right now."

"Why is that?"

"Because this whole thing took us by surprise and all of a sudden, my family was split apart. Now we are at the point where my wife doesn't bring the kids to see me anymore and I am having trouble dealing with that part of it, along with everything else."

"Oh, I'm sorry to hear that."

"Yeah, I know. She feels it is not a "good environment" for them plus wants to shield them from seeing me while I'm in here; at least that's what she says. I have a feeling it's something more than that and I can't get it out of my mind. It's been bothering me a lot lately and it just gets to me. She knows I am desperate to see them; it's almost like she's afraid something will happen to them if she brings them here."

"Well, certainly you can understand her concerns. Remember, she is trying to do the best for your children and sometimes, when we are put aside by our mate, it's very hard to understand and accept. Maybe you can suggest a different arrangement. Do you think that might convince her otherwise?"

"I'm not sure, she can be pretty stubborn sometimes. I've been married long enough to know that much."

"I'm married, too. I know exactly what you mean. They can be annoying sometimes, but we still love them."

"Yes, we do."

Don felt like he had to say that, even though things with Kate were now strained. He still loved her but he was worried that the love would turn into a one-sided relationship; he being the one doing the loving. Kate made no attempt to hide her feelings, or the lack of them. She told him straight out that her feelings for him had changed over the last few months. He no longer felt like her husband. It was almost as if he were her brother. That's exactly how she treated him. That fact alone gave way to her visiting him a lot less now and the visits came when there was a purpose to them; no longer did she come to visit and chat. Now her visits had a purpose and her coming to see him out of love and/or loyalty wasn't one of them. She was slowly weaning herself off him and even though they didn't talk about it, they both knew it. For her, it was a matter of self-preservation and self-respect. Did she really want to be known to everyone as the woman who still loved and supported her husband, even though he was accused of committing a sexual crime against their daughter? For Don, he knew it was only a matter of time before her love for him would be gone completely. He knew that day was coming, he just didn't know when. He worried about it constantly but yet he knew he was powerless to do anything about it. It was a constant source of stress for him. He wondered if he should have told the chaplain more than he did about the situation and how he felt. Maybe it would have helped if he had explained his feelings of anxiety in more detail. He didn't want to "hog" all of the chaplain's time, he did need to check in on the other inmates. He wasn't here solely for Don's benefit. The chaplain seemed more than willing to listen to Don, so maybe he would open up to him next time they spoke.

Unfortunately, there was plenty of time for that, he wasn't going anywhere. His acceptance of the plea offer made sure of that. Don just wasted away in jail, all of a sudden, he was barely a person, more like a human form, but not a complete man. He had no desire to take advantage of any of the activities available to him. He was depressed and the condition seemed to worsen each day, without Don knowing how to shake it. He didn't want to visit the jail library and pick up a book to read, he wasn't interested in taking any classes, etc. His days had developed into those where he was in a world all his own, and for now, he liked it that way. He did manage to eat because his appetite was still there but he never finished a full meal, he just picked at his food. Not only was he miserable mentally, but he was on his way to being miserable physically.

When you took into account his not getting any substantial physical exercise, his lack of intellectual stimulus from any source and his sparse food intake, it was only a matter of time before he would be in bad physical shape. The jail nutritionist did make a visit to him only last week to ask about the quality of the food. He said it was OK, and she said the reason she wanted to know what that she had noticed he wasn't eating much and she wondered if he felt it was due to the quality of food. He told her the food was fine but he wasn't much in the mood for eating a lot these days and it had more to do with his mood, not anything else. He asked himself why would she even care how much he ate or even if he ate at all? What was this, a hospital?

All Don wanted was to be left alone with only his thoughts to keep him company. If it was his scheduled time to go outside in the yard, all he did was sit alone on a bench. Other inmates played basketball but Don wasn't the least bit interested in that. He kept to himself and it made for a dull, boring existence only glorified by the gray walls around him. He was satisfied to exist that way, although it was a drastic change from the energetic and outgoing person he was when he was brought to the jail. Knowing he wasn't able to leave the jail for quite a while was really depressing to him and there wasn't much anyone could do to get him out of the funk he was in; those who knew him just accepted that's the way it was going to be until he was able to leave. Until then, he would probably remain in a deep depression and there was nothing anyone could do to change it, no matter how hard they tried.

Kate's reaction to his mood was one of ambivalence; in her weak moments she cared, during the rest of the time she didn't. She was the one left with everything, she was the one who had to care for the kids on her own and she was the one left with the responsibility of the house. Sometimes it was overwhelming and she thought she might crack, but then she would usually get a hold of herself and remember that she was the only one the kids had to depend on so she couldn't fall apart. She had to keep trudging on, no matter how much she wanted to stop and get away from it all.

The good mother, she could be; the good wife, she no longer wanted to be.

EPILOGUE

"Hey Mom, did you know that Dad has a girlfriend?"

"Really, when did that happen?"

"I don't know any of the details, just that he is living with someone".

"Well, since we've been divorced for five years, he can do what he wants with whoever he wants, but I will say I am surprised."

"Why? You have a boyfriend, so why are you saying that?"

"Because after all the trouble your father has had over the last few years, I would have thought he would want to be by himself. Get his life straightened out before he starts to be around someone else. He should just be careful, that's all."

"And here's something else."

"What else could there be?"

"Apparently this woman has three young daughters."

"Is he crazy? I am not saying he would try to do anything with those girls, but the woman he is living with may not know about his past. Someone needs to tell her."

"That might be true but I don't think that someone should be you."

"Probably not, but I would feel terrible if something did happen and I never told her."

"Mom, you'd better stay out of it. Why bring up all that old stuff again and get yourself all upset?"

"I'm not going to get upset, but maybe you are right. I can't protect everyone from him; that is not my job. Nor can I follow him around the rest of my life to make sure that he does the right thing."

"Exactly".

Kate knew Kara was right. It was hard to believe not that not all that many years ago Kara was a shy teenager and here she was blossoming into a lovely and confident young woman, who knew what she wanted from life and was doing her best to get it. Kate was proud of how she handled what she had been through and how she had gotten on with her life. You would've never know she had experienced the trauma she did in her young life, if you didn't know better. Kate knew she was lucky that it all turned out the way it did. It could have had much more dire consequences than it did. Somehow, all of them managed to dodge a bullet, from what Kara went through to having Don serve time in jail, which was plenty of time for them to get back to doing what they were good at, being a family.

Things had settled down into a nice relaxed pace for all of them, and they had waited long enough for that to happen. Now it was their turn at getting back some of the quality family life they deserved; the life that they had to give up suddenly. They were now minus one member, and they were doing fine with that, too.

Even the twins were doing well and seemed to be thriving. Tom was the more settled of the two, he had a good job with a bank and his business degree was being put to good use. He had just put a down payment on a small home not too far from Kate and Kara. He didn't want to be too far away from them, he felt that in spite of everything that happened, he wanted to be close to them. He knew they seemed to be handling things well by themselves, but who knew when the next shoe would drop. If it did, he wanted to be there. He was the more conservative of the twins, both in action and thought. He was going to be the one who was more like Don, stable, hard working and he knew how to manage his money. He was someone you could trust, if he told you he was going to do something, he did it. You always knew where you stood with him. He was dependable, yet easy going and liked to have a good time, but in a subtle way.

Tim was more of the party boy. He was living in a condo where there were always things going on in the complex and he was usually a part of the festivities. He had loads of friends and he always seemed to be on his way to some function or coming back from one. At a party, he was the one with the lamp shade on his head.

Yet, in spite of his antics, he had a soft spot for home and what it meant. Like Tom, he wanted to be near Kate and Kara. He took a different approach when it came to their safety. He was the one who wanted to be in charge, the one who wanted to run the show if something were to happen. You might not see or hear from him every day, but he could be found when you needed him. If you needed him, he'd be there. He might just want to run everything, when he did arrive.

Kara had decided to spend a few hours at the library, so Kate took a book and sat outside to enjoy the fresh air and warmth. Even the deck was a little warm to the touch, so she quickly slipped on her flowered flip-flops and sat in one of the patio chairs. She always felt so much better when she was outdoors, it was almost as if she was more alive somehow. Sometimes, she even brought her work with her to the back porch and was able to concentrate and get a lot done. That seemed to work well for her and the peace she found while doing it was good for her psyche. She was coping well, but she knew that she was only a fraction of an inch of losing it should something go wrong with Greg, now her boyfriend of five years, or the kids.

It seemed silly to refer to Greg as her boyfriend, after all, they weren't teenagers. He wasn't her husband, but he was so much more than just a friend. She guessed the boyfriend tag was OK for now, but there had to be a better term that was closer to describing what their relationship was. Until she could think of something more appropriate, boyfriend would have to suffice.

Kate figured she could stay outside for a few more minutes before having to drive into town to do some errands. She wanted to get done before Kara got home from the library. Kate was still in her "mother-mode" where if one of the kids was going to be there at the supper hour, then she was going to cook. Even if the kids insisted otherwise, that was the way it was going to be. She had decided to make Kara's favorite because she had a big exam in a few days and was truly worn out studying for it. Kate thought it would give Kara a nice break and would be something she would enjoy. Kate was still the ultimate care giver, the ultimate loving mother and the ultimate planner. The kids hated it when she treated them like they were still children, but secretly she found such joy in doing things for them. It made her happy and gave her a reason to spoil them.

Her thoughts were suddenly disrupted by the shrill ring of the cordless phone. She came to her feet to pick up the phone, which was on the patio table. She was hoping it was Greg, maybe she would invite him to have dinner with Kara and herself.

"Hello?"

"Hello yourself."

"Who is this?"

"This is Carolyn, a friend of your husband's."

"Oh? Well, first off, he is not my husband, he is my ex-husband. There is a world of difference and I like it that way. What can I do for you?"

"I don't know that there's anything you can do for me, but I called to tell you what a bum and piece of shit your husband is."

"I told you – it's ex-husband and however you feel about Don is really of no concern to me. Our marriage was over a long time ago, and since you are his live in girlfriend now, I don't know why you'd even want to talk to me."

"I'll tell you why, because your ex-husband is now in jail and I am 100% pissed about it!"

"Oh My God! What happened?"

"Well, it looks like we have more in common than we thought."

"What do you mean?"

"What I mean is that the jerk manhandled one of my daughters, that's what."

"Oh no............"

"Yeah? Try, oh yes and I am going to kill him myself as soon as I get close enough to him."

"Where is he now?"

"Oh, you don't have to worry where he is. I just called the cops and he is on his way to jail. He probably won't be out for awhile, but I thought you should know."

"Thank you for telling me, I would have heard eventually. What about your daughter? Is she OK?"

"Yeah, she's fine, she's just scared."

"The poor thing! Is there anything I can do to help you? Believe me, I have been there."

"Nope, I will handle it and my first job is to make sure the piece of crap never has anything to do with me again, or my girls. I will kill him if he does."

"I know what you mean. Damn! I thought he wasn't going to have any more trouble like this again. It is just so shocking...."

"Why is it so shocking? He's done it once, he can do it again."

"I guess so, you just hope he won't."

"Well, all I know is that I hope they throw the book at him this time. They don't need a criminal like him walking the streets. He is a danger to everyone around him. They need to keep him in jail and throw away the key."

"I am so rattled right now, I need to get on the phone. Please call if there is anything I can do for you."

"I doubt it, but it was nice of you to offer."

"Please call me if there is anything you need."

"Thanks, I'll be fine. It's Don who won't be if I have any say in the matter."

Kate hung up the phone and noticed that her hand was shaking.

She couldn't even believe what she had just heard! What could Don be thinking? Now it scared her to realize that during the eighteen years of their marriage that she hadn't known him at all! Yet, during those eighteen years, he'd never shown any signs of taking an interest in young girls. Where did that come from? No matter where it started or when, she knew the best place for him was exactly where he was headed. He couldn't be trusted. He had turned into her worst nightmare, it was all so degrading. No matter what, his actions were still a reflection of the family and they would forever be linked to what he did. It wasn't fair, life wasn't fair, but that's the way it was.

Kate was so shaken she didn't know if she should stay right where she was or go outside and start screaming to the neighbors. Should she call the boys? Kara would be OK until she got home. After all, Don was going back to jail, so there was no need to worry about his whereabouts. They were physically safe, but the mental state of it all was a different story.

The phone rang and Kate jumped. She picked it up and before she had a chance to start to speak, Greg spoke first.

"Kate, it's Greg. Have you heard the news about Don?"

"I just did a few minutes ago, his girlfriend called. She was more than glad to give me an earful."

"I am so sorry you had to hear it from her."

"Yeah, well if I had to hear it at all, I would say she would be at the bottom of my list. The nerve of the woman calling me, like I had something to do with it!"

"I don't think that's it at all. I imagine she just wanted to let you know and she is upset. You remember how it was when you found out about what happened to Kara."

"I know, but............"

"Listen, I am coming over to be with you for awhile. I have already called the twins and told them not to worry because I would be there. Where is Kara?"

"She went to the library."

"OK, well I'll swing by there on my way over and pick her up. I can bring her home with me and that way she won't have to drive. I would hate it if she were driving and then heard it on the news. That would upset her terribly and she should be with us right now. We don't know how she'll react."

"I know. But what about her car?"

"Don't worry, I'll let the twins pick it up or I will go back and get it later. We'll work it out."

"Greg, thank you so much, you are so good to me."

"There's no need to thank me, you know that. I am glad to do it for you and the kids. They deserve knowing they always have a soft place to land, and that is wherever you are. But if I have anything to say about it, I want to be there too."

"You are so great. OK, well go get Kara and I will be here waiting for you both."

Kate sat down on the sofa and tried to compose herself. She didn't want to appear to be visibly shaken when everyone got there and she was sure the boys would show up in not too long. She ran upstairs, splashed some water on her face, ran a quick brush through her hair and changed her blouse. She wanted to look freshened up, even though she felt anything but that way.

She went back to the living room and sat back down. Her thoughts drifted back to the day she was doing the same thing Carolyn was do-ing now, disbelieving it and being scared for her daughter at the same time. It brought back all the bad memories, all the bad days, all the bad thoughts. All of a sudden, Kate was thrown back in time, thrown back in a world she tried so hard to get out of. In the midst of it all, Kate was brought back to reality by the opening of the front door. It was Kara, followed by Greg. She hugged them both at the same time and the three of them were in an inpenetrable bear hug.

Soon after, the twins arrived, as she knew they would. All five of them were encircled in a long embrace, none of them wanting to let go, only imagining what they would have to go through once again.

Yet, at the same time, Kate felt a security she hadn't known when it happened the first time. Greg wasn't there to lean on, wasn't there to cry to and wasn't there to talk to. She needed all of those things, and for him, she was thankful.

But for her children, she was more than thankful. As she lifted her head to see all their four faces at one glance, she knew she now had everything she needed, and more.

CPSIA information can be obtained at www.ICGtesting.com
230437LV00001B/7/P